The Sebastian Handley Songbook

Lyrics, Chords & Assorted Thoughts

The Sebastian Handley Songbook – Lyrics, Chords & Assorted Thoughts

All Rights Reserved. No reproduction, copy or transmission of the publication may be made without written permission. No section of this publication may be reproduced, copied or transmitted without written permission or in accordance with the provisions of the Copyright Act 1956 (as amended). Copyright 2024 of the author. The right of Sebastian Handley to be identified as the author of this work has been asserted in accordance with the Copyright Designs and Patents Act 1988. A copy of this book is deposited with the British Library.

Amazon ISBN: 9798327469624

(REV250226)

First published June 2024

Most of these songs can be found on the Sebastian Handley Bandcamp site.

Cover image – John and Sebastian Thursday 18th January 2024.

3, Index
5, Forward
6, Songs
6, Country Girl
8, Lucky day
9, Scared of the Dark
10, Chinese Whispers
13, Rainy day
14, In the Morning
15, Silicone
16, Broken Heart
17, Sunrise
18, Midnight at the Feak Zone
19, Thin
20, Near
21, Scenes and Relationships
22, Hangover
24, Indian Summer
25, Crush
26, Weddings Make Me Cry
28, Flower Queen
29, Airplane
30, Live Together
31, Peace and Quiet
32, Rock and Roll
33, I Dreamt I Could Fly
34, Love One Another
36, Miguel Rodruigez
38, Big Love
40, Mexico
41, Numbers
42, Ballad of the Lonesome Rider
43, I Need Your Love
44, Get Happy
46, Let's Hang Out
48, Destination Planet X
50, Lord Nelson
52, Miss My Mrs
53, Alone Together
54, Marry Money
56, Mr. Average
57, Best Left Forgotten
58, Unknown Soldier
59, I'm a Lady
60, Miss Adventure and the Strangers
61, Kick and Run

62, Talking to Yourself
64, Lives of the Rich and Famous
66, Wake Up
67, Stop Pretending
68, Captain of the Ship
70, Creature of Habit
72, We Came From The Seas
75, Cheerio
76, Making Hay
77, Tomorrow Will Be Wonderful
78, I Hate Everything
80, True Love Express
81, Don't be a Cunt
82, Witchcraft
84, It Began With a Smile
85, Take Care
86, God Save the Queen
88, Money and Beautiful Women
89, Don't Worry About It
90, The Night is Young
91, Until We Meet Again
92, Same Shit Different Day
93, Fun Without Trouble
94, In the Summertime
95, Partied Out
96, Life is Short
98, OMFG
99, She Lives In Dreams
100, You Don't Need God to be Good
102, For Love or Money
103, Car
104, Home Sweet Home
105, Don't Send Messages When You're Drunk
106, Hooray for Cabaret
107, Young Again
108, Mr. Sunshine
110, Little Dreams
111, Wasting Time
112, She Only Blew My Mind
113, You and Me
114, Ones and Zeros
115, How Much Do You Need?
116, (I want a man that's) Good With His Hands
117, Washing Up

118, My Dream Came True
119, 'Girlfriend'
120, Head Honcho
122, We Are Together
123, Double Denim
124, Boy Meets Girl
125, The Sky is Blue
126, Food Shelter You
127, Chemistry

128, Delivery Man
130, Enough
131, Daddy is Best
132, Passing Through
137, Haikus
147, Photobooth
148, Bits and Bobs
154, What's best … ?
160, Timeline

Foreword

I'm only going to put brief explanatory notes about each song because, firstly, if the lyrics need a lot of explaining they are not worth explaining, and secondly because what you omit is as important as what you include. Moreover, current circumstances prevent me from being entirely candid about my youth, so I will just say that both joys and pains were extreme.

I am arranging the songs very approximately in the order in which they were begun. Some songs like '*Peace and Quiet*' or '*Alone Together*' were not completed till more than ten years after being started, but I'm going to prioritise the initial idea over the consolidation, which is why some songs appear early on even though I didn't record them till much later. This may seem odd, but it makes sense to me because they constitute landmarks. Because I write slowly there can be a considerable overlap between compositions, during which I remember, rethink and rewrite. A couple of early songs like 'The Garden' are omitted on the grounds of unoriginality and excruciating naivety; a couple of others like 'Fool' and 'Silly Fight' are omitted as inclusion could never cause more happiness than sadness.

What I got right was that I wrote as I learned. If I had postponed the writing till the learning was complete there would be no songs. As such the songs constitute a diary of learning - the early songs are nothing like the later ones. It's hard to appraise oneself, but I think the strengths are that I achieved a decent range of fast/slow, loud/quiet, happy/sad, melodic/dissonant, funny/serious, personal/impersonal compositions which were carefully constructed. I aimed high and only reined in my sincerity to spare others rather than myself. The weaknesses are:
1, I didn't write choruses in an age when the repetition was king.
2, My chords and melodies should have been more varied and muscular.
3, My musical performances were often under-rehearsed and technically ragged.
4, I was pig-headed about letting others produce the songs.
5, I self-imposed a rule of one note per syllable which precluded the idea of one syllable having a series of tones. Consequently, the songs often sounded like what they were –
poems set to music.

I do feel aggrieved at my lack of success. To this day no radio station has ever played one of my songs and no journalist ever reviewed my music (except Hej Doleman). Whist I accept responsibility for my failure, the failure also lies with those whose job it was to sort the wheat from the chaff. My job was to produce good work, theirs was to listen and apportion judgement; if only one of us are doing our job, there can be no meritocracy. So a big THANK YOU to those who gave me a chance and a big fuck off to those who didn't.

Regarding the curiosities at the end of the book, I am not cutting parts that I disagree with now because, again, they are chapters of a story. The timeline and notes mention people with a connection to the work and may therefore omit more important people who I didn't write about. This is the best I can do. I submit it to the judgement of the future.

Country Girl

She's a country girl
so I don't know why I'm falling in love with her
cos I'm a city boy
and city girls I usually prefer

…but not anymore I've fallen for…

A country girl!
I couldn't keep my feelings concealed.
I said to her:
"*I've had no experience in this field*". (no no)

I never saw the point of whistling sheep dogs
or '*getting down*' in peat bogs
but since we met I just wanna be hen pecked!

I'm a city boy
who used to watch the football match with palls
and she's a country girl
much more used to pulling bits of cows (ooo ahhh)

City girls know all the latest fashions
but she's got animal passions
and I'm all … ready for a woman who's primal!

And she's a country girl
who used to kiss the shepherd in the hedge
But I'm a city boy
and now she wants a slightly bigger wedge (yee haaa!)

She wants fax machines and calculators
I want home grown potatoes
Its a complete change of status! (get off my laaaand)

Chords:

Verse 1:
A D Dm A
A D Dm B
(D E D E)

Verses 2 and 3:
A D Dm A
A D Dm B E

Chorus:
D Dm A
D A
D E D B E

Notes: Circa 1996. Actually inspired by a lady who, although wonderful in every way, I have never been romantically involved with. In the days after leaving Gwent College (1990) but before the internet, I lost contact with my college friends but then somehow managed to get back in contact with my old chum Grace Horne. I was standing on the platform of Blackheath Station and in a moment of excitement thought *"She's a country girl!"* And as Louis Kahn would say *"the beginning confirmed the continuation"*. She will be amused and embarrassed in equal measure to learn that she inspired my first song. I can officially confirm we are completely unfamiliar with one another's fertilisers. Of all my songs this one has withstood the most stylistic interpretations. The punk version recorded by dum dum is one of the pinnacles of human achievement. The Chandeliers did a garage version and I sometimes play a comedy acoustic version at folk clubs. Maybe one day there will be a reggae death metal version – don't bet against it! The Chandeliers version features my dad (John Handley) and (future wife) Vicky making farmyard noises in the instrumental section. Also worth mentioning is that the best line *"it's a complete change of status"* was suggested by my dad. There is no question that this song is miles better than the Primal Scream song by the same name.

Lucky Day

It's my lucky day
just how I'd like it to be
Unhappy days are over
It's four-leaf-clover-ee!

It's my lucky day
couldn't ask for anything more
Bless my soul, things on the whole
are better than before.

Everybody likes to go dancing
everybody likes to kiss
everybody likes to fall in love
I like to sing about this!

It's my lucky day
just how I'd like it to be
I can't wait – everything's great!
I am really happy!

Chords:

Verse:
D D D D D B E A D (X2)

Chorus:
Bm7 D G F#m7
Bm7 D Em7 F#m7

Notes: I seem to remember the first line came to me when I received a dole check. I'm proud that the last word of the first verse rhymes with two different things.

Scared of the Dark

I'd like to leave you now and make my way to somewhere quiet and still
I'd like to take my rest, close my eyes and lie alone undressed
But I'm scared of the dark.

I'd like to wish you well, make my peace and dim the candlelight
I'd like to climb the stairs, reflect upon my day and say my prayers
But I'm scared of the night.

Six red flowers for one I love, for the half-a-dozen jewels I dream of,
Three for the kisses that sign your name, two for your lips, and one for love in vain.
I'm scared of the dark.

Verse baseline:
A A F E (x8) (In chords this is Am Am F Em)
E E E E G E G E G E G E E G (bent) E
B B A B BA

So basically, the verse is blues (1,4,5) using Am, Em and Bm

Tune:
Am Am Am F Em Em F Em
G G G F Em Em F Em

Notes: I had real trouble with the third verse which is silly as I had a good thing going with the first two and should have just done more of that. The recording with Dum Dum (Music City, New Cross again) is the sound of exploding amplifiers. It's precisely that sort of music that can only be played by young people. Recorded in one take with no overdubs on Sure 58 microphones, bleed everywhere, we smashed it.

Chinese Whispers

Sweet and sour flavours
music misbehaviours
were wayward in our labours
now were gonna wake the neighbours!

The fat cat's back to back-chat scat
prattle clap trap, pap on tap, tick my lick.
The dude-too-rude lures the pure
but's lost the plot too hot to stop – top or drop.
The sublimest crime is the nicest vice
so hoof the goof, skip the gyp, pit the wit.
The beat is meaty and the tone is droning
excuses are useless, my brain is absolutely polluted.

Its not coffee break time
halibut or skate time…
its not beef marinate time
its pussy on a plate time!

Dum Dum's dim din dumbs down no thumb's down
jumbled gibberish babbling gabble.
Perfect, Ben Hurr-fect, I blurt the dirt
slur absurd words spew blue rhubarb.
Fill with filth till the filth spills kill pills
feel till you've had your fill and feel ill.
Corrupt and fucked ruptured self-destruct
profane and caned – IT'S A BRAIN DRAIN!

We are playing coolly.
You are going drooly.
When girls around I'm cooey…
now dance like Hong Kong Phooey!!!

Chinese whispers and tongue twisters
my twisted shit's the pits, your brain blisters.
All the misses kiss the misters,
The gist is pissed – I twist the vistas.
ONE THING IS SOMETHING – BUT NOTHING'S ENOUGH
It's not art it's not smart it's just huff and puff,
but who's number one? Who's your chum? its Dum Dum!
…yum yum…in the tum…out the bum – done!

Music:
This is the fingering for the high blocks:

High E:
ooooooooooooX
ooooooooooooX
ooooooooooooX
oooooooooooo
oooooooooooo
oooooooooooo

High D:
ooooooooooX
ooooooooooX
ooooooooooX
oooooooooo
oooooooooo
oooooooooo

High B:
oooooooX
oooooooX
oooooooX
ooooooo
ooooooo
ooooooo

High A:
ooooX
ooooX
ooooX
ooooo
ooooo
ooooo

Last High E:
Open but you only hit the G, B and E strings.

… and here are the chords for the big noisy bits:

Big E:
oooooooooooooo
oooooooooooooo
oooooooooooooo
ooooooooooooX
ooooooooooooX
ooooooooooXoo

Big D:
oooooooooooo
oooooooooooo
oooooooooooo
ooooooooooX
ooooooooooX
oooooooooXoo

Big B:
ooooooooo
ooooooooo
ooooooooo
ooooooooX
ooooooooX
oooooooXoo

Big A:
ooooooo
ooooooo
ooooooo
oooooooX
oooooooX
ooooXoo

Final Big E:
ooooooo
ooooooo
ooooooo
oooooooX
oooooooX
ooooooo

Notes: In the mid-90s I had visited Blade in New Cross (I used to DJ for him under the name of Data) he showed me an idea for a track called Alphabet Slaughter which was great as it worked through the alphabet. I remember his last line was *"Extra, extra, You're a Zero"*. He mentioned another track he was working on called Chinese Whispers. I said I thought it was a great name for a song. He asked why, and I said because it could be clusters of spluttered vowel sounds rather than conventional rhyming. I later had a go and this is how it turned out. Many years later I joked with Blade about this, he said he couldn't even remember his track of the same name and that he was having crazy ideas for tracks every day back then. Maybe 'Not I' by Samuel Beckett was also an influence, as well as my ace chum Sue. Like 'Country Girl' there is a great punk version with dum dum and a later garage version with the Chandeliers. With the dum dum version, the guitarist (Rupert Anderson) was called *'Captain Frank Slime'*. In that recording for the second verse I sang *"Rocking is your fate Slime, it is not your break time"*. Also lost in the spluttered lyrics is the phrase *'nothing's enough'* which I consider to be the greatest two-word poem ever written.

Rainy Day

Rainy day, morning mid-September
Side by side in pale sunlight
Hurry home together.

Every Sunday, morning came to find us
With eyes wide open and ear drums ringing
Another night behind us.

Let's pretend, tell me how you need me
Breaking up is hard making up is easy
We could lie forever
Sharing precious moments close together.

Rainy day, mid-morning, September
Side by side as pale sunlight
lies with us together.

Let's pretend, tell me how you need me
breaking up is hard making up is easy
The sun came out to kiss you,
the stars come out at night because they miss you.

Chords:
Motif:
Em7 Bm7 Am7 Bm7 (x2)

Verse:
Em7 Bm7 Am7 Bm7
Em7 Bm7 Am7 Bm7
Am7 Bm7

Chorus:
Bm7 Am7 Em7 Bm7 (x2)
Am7 Bm7 Am7 Bm7

Notes: Circa 1996-7. A song about Colette. I had just moved into the basement flat of 27 Limes Grove in Lewisham. I had met her when I was working as a dishwasher, living at a squat in Hales Buildings at the Elephant and Castle. We would go clubbing somewhere like Cooltan in Coldharbour Lane or Brixton Academy take Es and wander home Sunday morning. The verses were about when we were together and the choruses were written when we were splitting up. The verses are more skilful than the choruses, but the last two lines of the song are very good. Wherever she is now I hope she is as happy as she made me. I honestly never thought of the similarity with *'There is a Light That Never Goes Out'*. Now I see it must have been an influence.

In the Morning

In the morning when soft light shines
sweetheart, sweetheart, and love's no longer blind,
where have all the stars gone? Where are all our dreams
sweetheart, sweetheart, when the sunlight streams?
Light that slowly changes, changed the night before.
Then I told you I loved, now, I love you more.

Now the roads are empty, thoughts are almost words
and nothing moves or makes a sound except the wind and birds.
Why do birds sing sweetly? Who can know for sure?
I don't even know what I'm trying to say, though I wish I'd said much more.
We are at the centre, we are in the sun
We are so much older, when the day is young.

Chords:
A C#m D
D C#m E
C#m D C#m D
A C#m D
D C#m A (x3)
A C#m D

Notes: A song about lying in the sunlight on a Sunday morning in Limes Grove. It was lovely how the light would come in the window. I'm proud of the last line.

Silicone

The don on song has got a claim to fame
I'm gonna think the brink, I'm gonna steam the cream
I've gotta rock the spot, until I waste the chaste
From when I split the tip, until I bend the end…

Silicone, beach and saccharine
lipstick mascara leopard skin
the fake stuff is better than the real thing
the fake stuff I prefer to the genuine…

I'm gonna smoke the roach, I'm gonna sink the drink
I'm gonna pill the ill, I've gotta feed the need
I'm gonna pop the top, I'm gonna stack the pack
I've got the most to boast, I'm gonna rule you all!

Silicone, beach and saccharine
lipstick mascara leopard skin
the fake stuff is better than the real thing
the fake stuff I prefer to the genuine…

(Optional 3rd verse used in 'For You' by the Dirge)

Low lights, high lights and silhouettes
Vodka, tonic and cigarettes
Sparkling jewels and a party dress
From the bar to the car, then the guiltiness.

Notes: Begun circa 1997. Living in Limes Grove Lewisham. I remember being very chuffed with the chorus, rhyming four multi-syllable words celebrating the artificial. I wish I had worked out better riffs for it. Almost any riffs would do as the words were just screamed. Looking back we should have adapted the Dum Dum track *'Oh Yeah'* for the music. Dum Dum recorded a version in music city that was miles too long. Years later Steve and I recorded it again for the Queen of Hearts album. This time shorter and with a riff that sounded less like Joy Division. But we just about made it to the end of the song - Rock and Roll is a young man's game and by then the wheels were coming off the wagon.

Broken Heart

When your heart is broken there's nothing you can do.
When your heart is broken it all comes back to you.
Fate is never kind, love is always blind
when your heart is broken in two.

When your heart is broken you dwell upon the pain.
When your heart is broken you think of who to blame.
You will never make that mistake again
when your heart is broken in two.

Why can't we be happy?
How were we so wrong?
And why do we have to accept these things,
and have to carry on?

When your heart is broken you want to be alone.
When your heart is broken nowhere is your home,
walk from room to room, but you are on your own
when your heart is broken in two.

Verse:
C F G (x2)
F G C F
F G C
C F G (x2)
F G C F
F G C C8

Middle:
F G C (x2)
F G C F
F C G

Note: About the split with Colette.

Sunrise

Love returns like sunrise
ascends and claims the heavens.
Let it shine, sun and stars be mine
broken, torn, try to carry on.
We are fools together
still two fall, forever in flight.

Dark the dawn that breaking
awakes me like a siren.
Give your heart, give it in your eyes
in the night, you and I arise.
Arise and shine your sleeper
sleep deeper, and let there be light.

Love returns un-silenced
demands its deeds and titles.
Sweet sweet sweet, kisses that we share.
hand in hand, give it all you can.
We are just beginning
when the stars are spinning through night.

Chords:
A Am G (x2)
Dm C Am Em (x2)
F Em (x3)
Dm

Notes: Circa 1998. After the split with Collette, Recorded at high tempo with Rupert and Steve for the first Dum Dum EP (called Silicone). Then many years later (after Rupert left) I re-recorded it with Steve for the '*Queen of Hearts*' album with a better tempo but worse guitar playing. I tried to sing '*let there be light*' the way Ian McCulloch sang '*you give yourself to him*'. I sang '*hand in hand*' quite well. The Chandeliers recording featured Milla on violin and Annie Ashton on cello. They also played on Airplane and Miguel Rodruigez.

Midnight at the Freak Zone

Midnight on the big night at the place were it's ace
It's the sublimest time now the hour must flower
Like the meaningful scene from the grooviest movie
Sweet and complete the Freak Zone peaks!

Baseline:
F# A C# A B B B C C# (x3)
F# A C# A B
A B A B A B
A A F E D D D D# E
A A F E D D D E D
A A F E D D D D# E
A A F E D D D E D
F# A C# A B B B C C#
F# A C# A B
A B C
C# C# C C B B A B A
F# (x7)
E F# F# F# F# F# F# F# (x3)

Notes: Circa 1997. Recorded at Music City with Rupert and Steve. Those were halcyon days when we felt we were in the greatest band in the world. I wrote the baseline, Rupert wrote a classic riff for it, and Steve arranged it into a coherent bit of music with beginning middle and end. It was our first ever recording session together. Me and Pert were desperate for Steve to drum for us. After this night of recording with Chris Mansell he was into it! Over the next 15 years Steve would go on to record numerous tracks with me. Writing this (in 2023) it's maybe been forgotten how most of the best stuff I have to show for my life would not exist were it not for his skill and thoughtfulness. He had the whole arsenal of what you would want in a musical collaborator.

Thin

I'm too thin, I'm too thin
I'm too thin, and I can't think
I'm too thick so I don't know
I'm too slow and I'm too slim.
Try to make good, try to make do,
try to come through and I try to stay clean,
but I'm too weak and it's too deep,
or its too steep and I'm too lean.

I can't wake and I can't sleep,
it's too dark and I'm too dim,
I'm too hard or I'm too soft,
I can't stay and I can't stray.
Try to make sense, try to make sure,
I'd die to be more and I try to stay cool,
but it's too late and I'm too straight
or I'm too pissed and I'm too small.

Notes: These lyrics were never recorded. No music was ever written for them. If it had been, the treatment would have been like Silicone or Chinese Whispers or Tourettes by Nirvana.

Near

I am near the end
I am near the end
try to define, draw a line
and step across again.
The dogs are barking at the water's edge
quiet reflections twist and shine,
I am in the darkest room,
life continues, things happen.

I'm not in control of this
but I won't change my course,
the river might be poisonous
but I am near its source.
I am near the end
I am near the end
let the gods come down on me
I can never bend.

Trying to make sense of this,
trying to make things fit,
it's all so significant
…if you think about it.
Some things are hard to talk about
some things are difficult to say
something is still and silent
but it never fades away.

Verse Chords:
Bm G#m Bm G#m
Em C#m Em C#m

Notes: I can't remember the chorus chords, but it doesn't matter as no one will ever play it. It's on the Boomerang album (disk two) if you want to look it up. Possibly about Collette. I've read about the symptoms of depression / bi-polar and they simply seem to describe normal human life. I always had 'depression' until I became a family man.

Scenes and Relationships

Scenes and relationships seem to draw me in.
They offer me a ride, so I get inside and they take me for a spin.
Let's go to a party, meet some people, make new friends.
We will dance together until this party ends.

Scenes and relationships always lead me on
They take me down, then they show me around, I always stay too long.
I am going deeper to see what's going down,
I'm trying to reach the bottom, of what goes round and round.

Love and happiness are just around the bend,
they call me away and they lead me astray, and they lead me home again.
We must press still further to see the things we are,
Love is getting closer when lovers go too far.

Chords:
Verse:
Am7 Dm7 Em7 Dm7 Am7 (x2)

Chorus:
Em7 Dm7 Am7 Dm7
Em7 Dm7 Am7 Em7

Notes: Circa 1998. I was deep in it at this time, keeping everything open-ended with girls. Exhausting myself pursuing as much pleasure as my conscience would permit, and sometimes a bit more.

Hangover

Down, come down,
wander round,
smoke another cigarette
and get all hung up on self-doubt.

Slow, so slow,
let it go,
write a list of things to do,
read it through, cross some out.

Watch the colours of the morning
dawning over me
things that happened since the sundown
I think about and comedown.

…comedown…
…comedown…

Close, so close,
kiss but then,
we will never meet again,
except in memories or dreams of party scenes.

Chords:

Verse:
Em7 Am7 Em7 Am7
Em7 Bm7 Am7 Bm7
Em7

Bridge:
E7 Am7 A* E7
E7 Am7 A*
Bm7 Am7 Bm7 Am7

The comedown section just bounces between these two chords:
I ooo
I xoo
I oxo
I oox
I ooo
I ooo

And this one:
I ooo
I ooo
I ooo
I oxo
I oox
I oox

The A* chord is basically all the strings open but playing a C on the B string like this:
I o
I x
I o
I o
I o
I o

Notes: Another song about being the worse for wear after a night of drugs and dancing. The chord change in the chorus is maybe the best bit of music I ever wrote, although the recording is so ragged it's hard to make out what notes I'm supposed to be hitting.

Indian Summer

Every year this time gets to me.
Plays upon my mind upsetting me.
Vows Spring makes the autumn breaks.

My love the flowers are dying
and soon their sweet perfume must fade.
Our world grows cold and drains colours
of paths and fields where we strayed,
but we still might have and Indian summer
before our nights close in.

My love our summer was squandered,
Now gone to play upon my heart
I watch the sky and I wonder
although the season grows dark,
we still might have and Indian summer
before our days grow dim.

Prepare your fires and shelters
As Earth's preparing its shroud.
We grow but only now we know the sunshine
now sunshine is breaking through cloud.
We still might have and Indian summer
before our nights close in.

Chords

Intro:
C Am Em (x2)
Dm F

Verse:
C Am Em (x3)
C Am G
Dm C Am G
Dm C G

Notes: First section recorded on a cassette round my mum's flat in Westcombe Park. Main body of song recorded at Music City with Steve and Rupert. Pert's slide guitar here was especially great.

Crush

I've got a crush on you
From the moment we first met I get
A kind of rush it's true
Anyone can tell I'm under your spell
I want a kiss with the one I love
I want a kiss with the one I love

I've got the hots for you
So exciting you ignite me and
You burn me up ooo yeah
It's insane I'm all aflame for you
I want a kiss with the one I love
I want a kiss with the one I love

Everything is cool and groovy
I see you looking so fine
Now that you're standing close to me
Im gonna make you mine!

I've got a crush on you
Since I saw you I adore you more
And every day I'll cry if you leave me
Please don't go believe me cos
I want a kiss with the one I love
I want a kiss with the one I love

Chords:
Verse:
G C Am D (x2)

Hook:
G C Am D
G C C Bm G

Middle:
Bm7 Am7 Dm7 G
Bm7 C Am D

Notes: Early days of being with Lucy. The chorus is maybe the best hook I ever wrote. I'm not at all surprised that I was writing songs like this and 'Near' and 'Thin' at about the same time, people have different moods.

Weddings Make Me Cry

Weddings make me cry however many I have attended.
I watch as the bride walks by to stand next to her intended.
Anything she wants to say, she's got to have it her way
She's the last to show, the first to go. This is her special day.

So you wish her every happiness,
and you say: 'it's a lovely dress'
She walks in with her father, out with her lover
she enters with one name and leaves with another.

So although I've seen it all before,
and I'll probably see a few more,
weddings are always sure to make me cry.

Preliminaries are gone through, possibly a reading too
Prayer or a brief citation, depends on denomination
The best man's face says it's all in place then it starts to get deep
With the promises – heavy promises – the promises you've got to keep.

See, we're all hoping and praying
that you mean all the words you're saying
'cos if you're not sincere – why are we here?
More dressed up than we've been all year!

But then two people agree
real happiness is being less free
so whenever the knot is tying
there's always a bridesmaid sighing,
and there's always some baby crying ... and me.

Motif:
C Dm Em
F G Em
C Dm Em
F Em Dm

Verse:
C Dm Em F C
F C Dm G
C Dm Em F C
F C F C Dm G
Em Am Em Am
F C F C
F Em Dm G
F C F C
F Em Dm

Notes: Took well over ten years to finish. A great bit of songwriting but I don't play it live these days because it's quite long. Many years later (around 2020) I attempted it at an open mic, a week before my mum was due to marry Jan Kot. Needless to say I had a bit of a blub and just about made it to the end - to the great amusement of the audience who thought it was part of the act. I probably got the idea from Kirsten Lyle telling me her favourite song was *'Nine out of Ten film stars make me cry'* by Veloso; also John Dawson married Sarah about this time. I was chuffed that I managed a 5-syllable rhyme (denomination) but also that no one would notice unless it were pointed out. I try to do this a lot now. I think it was Horace who said: *'the art is to disguise the art'*. Real happiness is being *less* free.

Flower Queen

I could look in your eyes till the stars fade at sunrise,
till the dawn is drawn by shadow, till the night bathes in moonlight.
We are touched, we are touching.
In our world, in our lives, we have hopes dreams and feelings,
choose our words, paint our pictures, meaning things, things that mean things,
till what's built up is broken
let it grow, let it grow…
All of our flowers have opened.
All of our flowers have opened.

I can't sleep, I can't wake, I can't think, I can't stand this
I can't heal, I can't help it, I can't form, I can't function
I can't fake, I am defenceless.
We press on, we continue, walk our paths, give our reasons,
play our games, take our chances, act our roles, make our choices,
and lose our minds to our senses.
We get high, we get high…
and break like the waves of oceans,
break like the waves of oceans…

Intro and end:
G C G C

Verse:
G Am Bm Am (x2)
Bm Am

Chorus:
Bm B
C Em Bm Am
C Em Bm Am

Notes: The age of Lucy.

Airplane

In my life with all its complications
I can't wait forever to make life's big decisions.
I want to fly and airplane,
I'll fly an airplane … leave all this behind me.

We'll find somewhere the sun is always shining,
We won't ever touchdown, we'll just keep on climbing.
I want to fly an airplane
I'll fly an airplane … somewhere I'll be happy.

Cleared for take-off, what if we get too high?
Live among the stars with me, and fly
fly…fly…

Verse
Em7 Bm7 (x4)
Am7 Bm7 (x2)
Em7 Bm7 (x2)

Middle section:
Am7 Bm7 (x3)
Em7 Bm7

Notes: Looking back maybe this was influenced by *'Fly me to Brazil'* by Astrid Gilberto. When I was young my dad used to sing the Songs of Travel by Vaughn Williams which I still like now. My first travel song.

Live Together

We can't go on year after year torturing ourselves like this.
We can't go on living on the run, chasing after happiness.
Someday something's got to happen that makes everybody change sides,
and someday we've got to stop running and jump across the great divide.

Because we can't go on like rats in a cage, playing on a wheel to get by,
If we can't get on, then what we gonna do when we have to get along or die?
Someday we've got to look forwards and put all the pain behind,
and some day we've got to be forgiving and expect some forgiveness in kind.
Before we lose our minds, we've got to live together.

It's alright to love - there is nothing wrong with love or answering somebody's prayers.
It's alright to kiss - if your old enough to kiss and it doesn't hurt someone that cares.
If all of our vows are broken and all of our promises are lies
then how can we hold our arms open and look into somebody's eyes?
We can only rise when we can live together
Live together
Live together
In love.

Intro:
G C G C

Verse:
G C Cm G
G C Cm D

Bridge:
C D G C (x2)
D
C G C D

2nd Bridge
C D G C (x2)
D C G C D
C G C D
C D

End: G

Notes: A song about harmony, compromise and finding meaning in human terms. I remember I had a flurry of lyrics for this whilst working at Halpern Partnership in Old Street with Jezza. I was just about to move to Koln to be with Lucy who had just started Saturday Night Fever. Builds like a wave from acoustic, to pop, to instrumental. I was a functional guitarist but a decent bass player so for the recording (many years later) I played the final solo on a de-tuned bass guitar which I think was a nice idea. Steve and I recorded it live, then I overdubbed the bass. I like the recording.

Peace and Quiet

Now it is time for peace and quiet
as the centre of town falls still.
For now we must stop and shut up shop
get our bags and cash up the till.
I'd have loved to have spent this day with you
in the season of peace and goodwill.
All the work this year is done
and the drinking has begun,
so God bless you, and everyone.

Now we reflect on years gone by
and the things that our loved ones said,
and look forward to what we plan to do
in the years that remain ahead.
I'd have loved to have spent this day with you
but my thoughts are with you instead.
So I'll wish you all the best
and I'll say to you 'God bless'
may your days be filled with happiness.

Chords:
G
C G D
C D G D
C G C G C G
C D G

Notes: I was in Koln, Germany 2000. It was a happy time. In Britain there is always some shop open, so for a Brit in Germany it's a shock how everything suddenly switches off on Christmas Eve. I had been shopping and suddenly found myself in a ghost town then I thought *"of course – now it's time for peace and quiet"*. I fiddled with it for years till I was happy with it. Now as an atheist I'm slightly irritated by the religious bits but I'm not going to rewrite again. Its precise. I did good work here. Maybe my most perfect song.

Rock and Roll

I just wanna rock and roll with you
I just wanna give you love so true.
Cool baby now here I am!
You are the one and I'm the man
Groovy now groovy now make it all right
I wanna rock and roll with you tonight!

I just wanna make your dreams come true.
Rules are the walls were breaking through.
Swing baby and spin in time,
all I wanna do is make you mine.
Queen of the scene and star of this show
make up a dreamy team now let's go!

You and me want to get together
and stay together all night long.
Were gonna fall in love forever
and how could that ever be wrong?

I love you; you love me too!
Were all cool now what you gonna do?
Since we met we want to get down
jump to the front and paint the town.
You're the first choice and it's the last chance
so forget other men you met and let's dance!

Verse:
D Bm D Bm
G D Bm
A G D

Chorus:
G D Bm
G A

Notes: Still in Koln. This song came to me in a dream. Years later I realised that '*Rave On*' by Buddy Holly must have been in my subconscious. To make matters even worse the chorus sounds like '*This Old House*' by Shaking Stephens! Lucy said the singing sounded like a howling dog on a veranda.

I Dreamt I Could Fly

Dim the lights that I might look on sunny days.
Dim the lights that I might look on ocean waves.
Last night it happened once again
and last night it happened just the same.

So bring the night for darkness makes it clear to me,
draw the blinds for blinded it draws near to me.
Last night it happened once again
I was down, Earth bound I ran and then,

I dreamt I could fly
I dreamt of a cloudless sky
and the birds became my friends
and showed me secrets of the heavens.
Beyond the seas
upon the breeze
I dreamt I could fly.

Everyone must dream and everyone must wake up,
spread their wings and turn their minds to higher things.
It was real, as real as you and me,
I was chained, contained but I broke free,
and I dreamt I could fly.

Verse:
Em G Bm D (x2)

Bridge:
Am Bm D (x2)

Chorus:
G Am Bm C
Bm C Bm C
Bm Am Gm F#m Em

Notes: I kept trying to write a song that began with five syllables like '*I Fought in a War*' by Belle and Sebastian. I didn't get very far with it till I moved the five-syllable phrase to the beginning of the chorus. The last verse isn't the same standard as the rest of the song. The dum dum version was an epic (ref Echoes by Pink Floyd). I re-recorded a garage version with the Chandeliers, changing the last verse to:

What foreign lands by night our own minds lead us through.
What distant shores and magic worlds they take us to.

… Passable, but rhyming '*to*' and '*through*' is nothing to write home about. Often my second verses are better to my final verses. Endings are hard.

Love One Another

Why be so uptight, when we could love each other?
And why stop and say goodnight, when we should love each other?
Everybody's got to change sometime
and when's the best time we should start?
Maybe here tonight will see the one time
that you let the sun shine in your heart.

People of the world agree and get along together.
Let your minds and your hearts run free and get it on together.
Let's count every star that's shining
and give every one of them names.
Let's take off and never stop climbing
till we go down together in flames.

But I'm shot – I'm all strung out
and my heart is hanging on a string
so love one another all you can, and let it in…

I dreamt about the years that had passed and felt them weigh upon me.
And the moments that I tried to make last but had to watch slip from me
I want to set this out in every last detail
so that everybody after can see
and pass time again with people who in time passed,
and have everything that never can be,

and get high – until it all comes down
to the only thing that's left you can't doubt…
love one another all you can
love one another all you can
love one another or be damned
and let it out…

Music:

Independent tune:
G
Am C Bm
C Bm G
Bm C

Verse:
G Em Am D
G Em Am D

Bridge:
Am D G Em
Am D Em Bm

Chorus:
C Em Bm Am
Bm Am

Structure:
T, V, B, V, B, C, T, V, B, C (repeat Bm & Am) T, T

Notes: Started towards the end of my time in Koln. Features what I call an '*independent tune*'. We were drinking in a bar, in Chlodwigplatz and I thought '*why be so uptight?*' A happy chapter of my life was drawing to a close.

Miguel Rodruigez

Miguel Rodruigez is watching his back
and his mind tracks back to the day before,
as he walks through the rain in the night and returns to the scene...

And Miguel Rodruiguz is watching his step
though each step takes him further from certainty,
until he stands by the motel door where the murder has been!

And he tries not to make any sound
as the handle on the door turns round,
he sees the body on the bed in blood
and the key to the safe on the ground!

Miguel Rodruigez is holding his breath
scared half to death of the consequence,
he walks across the room real slow, drawing his gun.

And Miguel Rodruigez he thinks his luck's changed
as he picks up the key and he looks at it,
he's been a loser all his life and at last, his moment has come...

But then he hears the door close behind,
and he sees all along he's been blind.
He's been cheated, double crossed and he's cursed...
someone else had got to it first!

And he looks in the face of the man who was once his best friend.
As he looks in the eyes of the last one to stand in his way.
Taking aim for the heart though he's shaking and at his wits end.
He puts his finger on the trigger of his pistol and...
...wonders what as he dies he might say...

Motif:
Am C Am G (x2)

Verse:
Am
G F E

Chorus:
G Dm (x3)
E

End:
E F G C Dm
Dm Em F Am
E F G C Dm
Dm Em F Am
E F G C Dm
Dm Em F Am
G F E

Notes: Back in London and somehow managed to reunite Dum Dum for a swansong. Third person storytelling makes a refreshing change to 'me me me' songs. My first cowboy song, written just before 'Lonesome Rider' and 'Mexico'. A bit like how the Beatles did Daytripper and Paperback Writer at the same time and then moved on. Joe said he liked the ambiguity of the last line (we are not sure which '*he*' is being referred to) but I saw that as a weakness.

Big Love

Big love (yeah)
A big love (yeah)
Its alright, its alright
it's all night, and so right

that I like it
I excite it
I cant wait
it's too late
I can't stand
or think straight

and its cool
cool…

Its too pure (yeah)
but you lure (yeah)
I woo woo, now guess who!
It's just you! It's all true!

There's no time
so be mine…
The diseased brain burnout craze!
The love boat stowaways!
The speed freak runaways!
The love drug danger phase!

it's cool
yeah cool…

I'm not sure (yeah)
but want more (yeah)
confused brain
confused pain
The fast car
the last bar
and its cool
cool…
cool…

Riff
E D B A E

Chorus
G Em Bm F#m

Notes: Musically unoriginal but the sort of thing that me Pert and Steve were good at smashing out. The verse was just a mash-up of LA by the Fall and Penetration by the Stooges. When I was young, I tried to sound like those I admired, but as I aged, I sounded more like me. The band practice version recorded on a cassette tape was electrifying. I'm pleased with the audaciousness of the lyrics. One of the last Dum Dum recordings. I think we did it around 2002 after I came back from Germany.

Mexico

Closed is my heart and cold is my sentiment far from the land I love.
Closed is my heart and cold is my sentiment far from the land I love.

Notes: The outro music of this song later got recycled into the Dirge song 'Imposter'. Similar pace and baritone as Lonesome Rider.

Numbers

Many a flower must bloom unseen.
Many a dawn forgets nights dream.
When the summer's done and the leaves fall down
all that remain are evergreen.

How many times will the ocean roar?
How many pebbles are on the shore?
Every one I take and throw into the sea
wave after wave returns to me.

At night I think about numberless things and numbers,
but however much I calculate the numbers always seal my fate.

How many flowers will bloom in spring?
How many birds in summer sing?
Will anything be shown? Will everything be known
before the leaves upon the breeze are blown?

At night I think about what I must do before I'm through,
but when I wake and see the day the nightmares all seem far away.

Verse:
Am7 Dm7 Am7 Em7
Dm7 Em7 Dm7 Am7

Chorus:
Em7 Dm7 Am7 Dm7
Em7 Dm7 Am7 Em7

Notes: My mum said she had seen a production of King Lear where the fool was like a George Formby type character, singing his lines whilst playing a Ukelele. That got me thinking. My dad liked this one.

Ballad of the Lonesome Rider

I am the lonesome rider,
many miles have I roamed.
Go state to state
but nowhere is my home.
I am the haunted outcast,
many lands have I known,
but I was born to live and die alone.

Gaze across the mighty canyon and I remember you.
I think about the way that your eyes flash as you smile.
Maybe I'm a fool for not returning back to you,
but returning back has never been my style.

Ride through the darkened forest…
Ride across the central plane…
and the twisting path across the mountain range
Think about the way you kissed me…
think of how our love was blind…
and I think about what I have left behind…

Look into the flames of the campfire and I remember you,
look up to the sky and I see a shooting star.
Look upon the path I know would lead me back to you…
until I look inside and know I've come too far.

Verse:
Am A* Dm C
Am E Am
E G

Chorus:
Dm Am (x3)
Dm Em

The A*chord is a weird but good chord dreamt up by Rupert:
It's basically Am but you flatten the A string by one semitone. Try it, you will like it:
Ioooox
Ioooox
Ioooox
Iooooox
Iooooox
Ioooox

Notes: Character study in which the backward path is considered, rejected, and the awful consequences accepted. The recording by the Chandeliers features my dad playing the mouth organ. Steve overdubbed the clip-clop sound with coconut shells.

I Need Your Love

I need your love. I need your love,
like I need the sun and rain.
Touch me once and make me young again.

I need your kiss, your tenderness
count the stars in the sky with me,
climb the mountain peak and fly with me.
I need your love.

You have cast a spell on me,
every act every hour all tell on me.
Look into my eyes, I won't compromise
say the word, set me free.

I need your touch, you love so much
I can't think of another thing,
there's no sense and there's no reasoning
I need you touch.

All of my life I've been wandering,
am I hoping for what never can be?
Look into my eyes, I won't compromise
say the word, set me free.

Chords:
Am Dm Em Dm Em Dm (x2)
Am
Dm Em (x3)
Am

Notes: Not much to say about this. Weird that I ever wrote something that sounds like a power ballad. Now I cringe a little that I didn't try something more ambitious than rhyming '*be*' with '*free*'. A couple of fun facts re the Queen of Hearts album ... The makeup artist for the artwork shoot was Dominic Skinner who would later on go on to be a celebrity makeup artist on *Glow Up*. The photographer, Kelly, later married Richard Strange from the Doctors of Madness.

Get Happy

Mr. Love is coming your way!
…His jet is taking off today,
and he's gonna drop a love bomb
with all of the bells and whistles on!
He told me I should say to you
that you only wash up when he cooks,
I feel I should convey to you
he's noted for his looks,
he's always kind to animals
and he's even read some books!
…so GET HAPPY!

He's got a big surprise
and it's gift wrapped and it's super-sized,
and you've got a treat in store
when Mr. Love knocks at your door
he's got you Persian kittens
and some shoes from your favourite shop.
He's taking you to Gareth Pugh
to spend until you drop.
And his house is like the Eiffel Tower
and the bedroom's at the top!
…so GET HAPPY!

He's got you flowers and a wedding ring
and a panda from Shanghai Zoo,
a silk embroidered dressing gown
with Belgian chocolates too.
and he's got a great big rocket ship
to take off in with you!
…so GET HAPPY!

Verse:
Em7 D Bm7 (x2)

Bridge:
C Am7 Em7 D
C Am7 Bm7
C Am7 Em7 Bm7

Chorus:
Em7 D Em7 G D
Em7 D Em7 Bm7 Am7

Chorus baseline:
E E D D E D E D E D
G G A G F# F# A F# D
E E D D E D E D E D
B B D B A A B A G E

Notes: For years I had a baseline that was nice and melodic. It reminded me of the Cure. I eventually managed to build a song on top. I would like to think that one day Gareth Pugh might hear it and smile.

Let's Hang Out

Let's hang out, let's hook up,
kill some time in town,
check out what's going down.

Look me up, fit me in.
Rendezvous tonight,
hit some bar, alright
let's hang out.

I figured it might be cool
if we check a party out one time.
Instead of just hang about
we should let it all hang out sometime.

Nice conversation, no complication
and I kind of dig the way the thing grooves
and I'm into how you do that dance moves
cool situation.

'cos everything you do rocks
and reminds me of a thing that I missed
you really tick my box,
we should hang out all the time like this.

Verse:
Am Dm Em Dm Em Dm (x2)
Am

Chorus:
Dm Em Am
Dm Em F

Tune (Same as Weddings Make Me Cry):
C Dm Em
F G Em
C Dm Em
F Em Dm

Notes: A song about indecision. We are presented with a bet-hedger trying to hint their way to happiness. My dad would also often write songs about imagined perfection, another time, another place, if only things were different. The demo was electrifying, I was convinced it was a hit, but the finished version didn't excite me as much, I'm not sure why. I recorded a version with Shirani Boelee and Ed Hoskin. Shirani did her best with it and sung it brilliantly, but the composition wasn't really finished at that time. I fucked up by asking them to work on half-baked material. It was always a struggle to finish this composition. It's about longing, and it has its strengths, but I will always see this song as the one that got away.

Destination Planet X

It's destination Planet X
where everybody just has sex,
where it's all fun that's just begun,
and there's no guilt and no regrets!

It's destination Shangri-La
where no joke ever goes too far,
and everyone's a movie star
playing Beatles' songs on Gretsch guitar!

We're gonna hang where porn stars bang
where beer is cold and no one's old.
Where nothing has no consequences
its all cool – and there's no fences…

It's destination El Dorado
where I just nob Nelly Furtardo
in the pink and in the stink
with chicks with dicks and Brigitte Bardot!

It's destination masturbation
where life is one big, long vacation;
where freedom is just free for me
and selfishness is liberty.

We're gonna chill with time to kill,
where there's no pain and there's no blame
and there's no war and no one's poor
and all of the people is really equal.

There will be no compromise after the hip revolution.
We got ourselves a real hero, we're off to year zero
where nobody works and nothing hurts;
a grand final solution – a new Jerusalem…

So it's destination Planet X
where everybody just has sex,
where it's all fun that's just begun
and there's no guilt and no regrets!

Verse:
Gm A#
Gm F
Gm A#
Dm Cm Gm

Chorus:
Cm Dm

Middle:
Gm Dm
Cm Dm (x3)
Gm F Gm

Notes: Mocking existentialism, idealism and myself. I wrote the first four lines in College Café at the top of Loampit Hill around 2009. I haven't played it live for years but when I did I left out the middle section as it isn't good enough. My contempt for interior-centric philosophy would later be set out in '*Brexit, Kant and Othello*'.

Lord Nelson

I want to die how Nelson died
knowing that the job was done.
And I want to cry how Nelson cried
knowing that the battle's won:
"thank God I've done my duty"
I thank God I got my duty done.

So the hour I fall at the boatman's call
want my family out of harms way.
No song and dance or fuss at all
just a friend at hand to hear me say:
"thank God I've done my duty –
`thank God I finished what I had begun"
…because when the shit goes down…

I don't want to die with an ache still in my heart.
I'm scared I'm going to leave things unfinished that I start,
and when I meet Grim Reaper he's going to take his scythe
and rip me all apart.

So I try and do what I think's true
but there's no true path you can take.
Wherever it leads it also leaves
the road you've got to forsake.
The only truth is beauty.
Beauty is truth and all that's left is doubt.
…There must be someway out…

I want to lay me down in a quiet restful place.
But ill go like a wretch, blaming all for my regrets,
and kick and scream and splutter
till I look up and see Lord Jesus' face.

Chords:
Am7 F E (x2)
Dm7 Fm7 Am7
Em7
Dm G C Am
Dm G C A
Dm7 Fm7 Am7

Notes: So I had done cowboy songs (Miguel, Mexico and Lonesome). Next came sailor songs, so we can lump this one with *'Captain of the Ship'* and *'We Came From the Seas'*. I suppose that whereas the cowboy songs present loners doomed by their decisions, sailing is about navigating a ship - working together for the best. This song asserts that true enrichment requires sacrifices and that there is no perfect path. I was born on the 21st October, the anniversary of the Battle of Trafalgar and the day Nelson died. I was very Christian at the time. Milla said she thought this was the best thing the Chandeliers ever did. It would be a bit embarrassing for me if people thought I never topped this song after I became an insufferable atheist bore. The recording is good but only hints at how much this song blew the roof off when the Chandeliers played it live. My singing on the recording is poorly phrased - the syllables should have flowed like water.

Miss My Mrs

I want to be the only one…
I don't want to be the lonely one…
God knows how hard its getting … phew!

Every night I think of her and I wonder where it will end.
So every day I wake and ask myself: "Will the pain ever mend?"
It's no good to get yourself all uptight,
but when a chick is so out of sight
all that I can do is hope I make it through the night.

So I get up and wash myself and I put my shirt and tie on.
Drink my coffee and go to work now I've got to try to be strong.
But I just want to shout it out loud and clear:
"all I want is holding her near"
I pace across the floor, I can't wait anymore till she is here…

I miss my Mrs. I miss my Mrs.
It is an actual fact whatever it may have lacked
I still want all her kisses.

so I want to set the record out straight
life's too short to h-h-h-hesitate…
until she is with me…its insanity!…but I CAN'T WAIT!

I miss my Mrs. I miss my Mrs.
no matter where she has gone, whatever she has done wrong
I want to fulfil her wishes.

I'm craving misbehaving. I'm fretting for the petting.
I'm hurting for my skirting, awaiting fornicating…
…God knows how hard its getting…
…it's it's it's not fair!

Chords:
F#m
Bm F#m Bm F#m
Bm C#m

Notes: I was thinking about the Ertha Kit song '*Where is my Man?*' and how the song might be if the genders were inverted. What would I miss? Mrs. Hallmark audaciousness. Chandeliers did a great job making it sound a bit like Remain in Light (Talking Heads). Maybe my first 'contradiction song'.

Alone Together

Into the void, the infinite, from our open hearts and eyes
To where all good I ever done is forgotten
Darling I love you more than I can say
and whatever happened yesterday
does it really matter here today?

Alone together at last,
far from their eyes and judgements and scorn
As secrets of the past are awoken from their sleep
And all the words we never said are spoken
And we are far away from everyone
In a moment we are old and young
And do everything we wish we'd done

My love, my sweetheart, my friend
Till sweet excess consumes us and fades
More love more love, more everything we're two ripples in the sea
And we go on and on until it's over
Although the moments in themselves are short
Even if they all amount to nought
Somewhere there's a place forever
We are alone together.

Chords:
Fm G# Cm x 2
Bbm G# C#
Bbm G#
C# Cm C# Bbm
Cm C

Notes: Very hard to place this song chronologically. I worked out the first few chords when I was with the Chandeliers in the big practice room at Cybersound (Deptford) when we were recording Miss my Mrs (2007). I don't know if I ever really managed to successfully resolve the cycle of chords. I ended up doing the minor, to major, then back to the beginning thing which worked ok; but I'm not sure the last chords of the cycle are as compelling as the first ten. I knew from the feel of the music that the words would have to be of searing intensity and that I would have to write in a completely different way to every other song. The feeling for the middle bit came to me in a lift in Goodge Street underground station. I made pages of notes over many years, most of which were discarded. Consequently, we have something that has emotive power, but ambiguous subject manner. I first played it live at the Constant Service pub (2024) and it went ok but it's rather intense for an open mic situation and I'm not really sure what others make of it. It's a shame the Chandeliers are no more as Milla, Joe and Steve would have turned this into a monstrous piece of music. I always imagined a long instrumental beginning with each instrument dropping in and out at significant moments. The words slip in sideways at the bridge rather than the verse.

Marry Money

Your meditation's much too transcendental,
your quest for happiness too existential.
If you're seeking meaning in existence
first you need some financial assistance!....

If you ever want to be happy, you've just got to know one thing:
find some dunce that's loaded, and get them to wear your ring!
Marry money child of mine and the rest is a turkey shoot,
just mouth those vows and then your spouse will have to part with loot....

...now I'm going to tell you about Aunty Mary....

Aunty Mary she was prone to serial bed-hopping.
If you saw the things she did your eyeballs would be popping!
For a lovely pair of shoes her draws would soon be dropping,
she doesn't love her husband....BUT SHE SURE DOES LOVE THE SHOPPING!

So marry money child of mine and the rest is a piece of cake.
(Once that home is half your own you don't need no career break)
and have some lazy selfish kids that do less work than bums on skids
and make it clear they've got no brains by giving them real dopey names...

...like (insert celebrity child name here)?

...now I'm going to tell you about Uncle Fred...

Uncle Fred was prone to wed cunning little schemers,
once he walked 'em up the aisle they took him to the cleaners!
He was working day and night until he looked beat up,
now he takes it up the flue but he can put his feet up!

So marry money child of mine and the rest is a Sunday stroll,
you get more cash than those who work and you live like you're on the dole.
So make that fund your husband and make that home your wife.
Get married...
...and then get divorced...
...and then...get on with your life!

Intro:
D G A D
D G A D

Verse (x3)
D A
A D
D G
A D

Notes: Some gold here! The Unkle Fred verse absolutely takes the piss, but unless I can write a better line for *'lazy selfish kids ... dopey names'* I won't bother playing it again.

Mr. Average

Hello I'm Mr. Average.
I'm just your average guy,
medium build moderately skilled
I give life my average try.
And nobody saw me walk in here
and no one's going to see me leave,
and in the hour of my death I'll draw my last breath
and no child of mine will grieve.

Because I'm the middle man – the second fiddle man,
the shadow, the saddo the also-ran.
Just biding my time and standing in line,
counting my days and set in my ways.
I put one foot in front of the other
and I watch everybody pass by,
and I huff and I puff and I talk about stuff
because, I'm just your average guy.

How d'ya do? I'm Mr. Nothing's True
(it depends upon your point of view)
Hello, I'm Mr. I Don't Know,
don't ask me – I go with the flow.
There ain't no use and no excuse
for the way that my day's panned out,
I just wait in the wings and analyse things
till the only thing that's left is doubt.

Good afternoon I'm Mr. Someday Soon
one day I might write one good tune
that begins on the wings of a new sensation
and ends like The Book of Revelation.
But I waste time so time wastes me
as I count every hour pass by,
I ain't no great shakes, bet no high stakes
see, I'm just your average guy.

Chords:
Gm A#m Gm A#m Gm
Cm Dm Cm Dm

Notes: I started writing this around 2008. I read an article by (I think) Simon Barnes, about a former Man City goalkeeper who died in the Munich air crash. I felt strangely emotional and wrote this song mocking myself. The Chandeliers played this really well.

Best Left Forgotten

Imagination's a wonderful thing, no denying it.
What joy could life bring if you aim high in it?
Well I know it's pretty rotten but not every dream begotten
works out, so some are best left forgotten…

Things that might have come true can weigh down on you,
missed some boat now there's a big frown on you.
You're in the middle of nowhere, that's when I say WHOA THERE!
Maybe it is best not to go there…

The loves that might have been, the places never seen,
the houses and the money, your nightmare is your dream.

Possibilities are endless in the world today
so the reason why I penned this is to try to say
it's very hard I know when your heart might overflow
but sometimes it is best to let it go…
Sometimes it is best to just let go…

Chords
Fm7 Gm7 Cm7
Fm7 Gm7 Cm7
Fm7 Gm7 G# A#
Cm7 Gm7 Fm7
Fm7 Gm7 Cm7
Fm7 Gm7 Cm7
Fm7 Gm7 G# A#
Cm7 Gm7 Cm7
Fm7 Gm7 G# A#
Cm7 Gm7
Fm7 Gm7 Cm7
Fm7 Gm7 Cm7
Fm7 Gm7 G# A#
Cm7 Gm7 Cm7
Cm7 Gm7 Cm7

Notes: Carefully constructed and upbeat. I think I played it once live. It didn't bomb but I always had better songs so it got mothballed.

Unknown Soldier

As time moves on and I am gone
please light a candle for me.
To mark what's passed recall I asked
you light a candle for me.

No one will recall my name
and no one will recall my face,
but please remember what I did
when I am in my resting place.

I never made the home parade
but shed my blood in foreign mud.
I never reached the highest ranks,
or ever heard a word of thanks.

But in my life I fought for you
and at my death I thought of you,
so say a payer and love me true
and light a candle for me.

Chords:
C F G
C F G
F G C F
F C G
C F G
C F G
F G C F
F C
F G C

Notes: I was at CZWG and living at Halesworth Road when I did this. So maybe I wrote it about 2008?

I'm a lady

Can't you express the way you feel to me?
Can't you say anything that's real to me?
We are hanging out together, been going steady sometime,
but are you ever gonna be ready to say you're mine?

A woman needs a man that's straight with her,
not hedge his bets and hesitate with her.
We can carry on whatever, but I just want to be clear
just where do you want this thing to go from here?

Cos I'm a lady
I'm a wallflower.
You've got to treat me like a lady
if you want me to treat you like a man.
You must respect me,
persuade me,
before you can expect me
to show you everything that I am.

But you chase everything that's far away,
and can't love anything that's here today.
Tell me what do you believe in?
Tell me that you love me alone,
or else tell me it's time you're leaving
to be on your own.

Verse:
A C#m D (x2)
Bridge:
Bm C#m D C#m Bm E

Chorus:
A Bm C#m D
A Bm C#m D E

Notes: I wrote this when the Chandeliers were still going. Milla didn't want to sing it which is a shame as she would have smashed it. I had a go, but it was never properly recorded. I think there's a good demo version on Youtube. Another lecture to myself. My memory isn't great but I think I proposed to Vicky shortly after writing it.

Miss Adventure and the Strangers

We got the bass … and the drums
And electric guitar now here it comes
We are Miss Adventure and the Strangers
With a truck load of messed up trash.

We take the words … and the tune
And put it together with a BOOM! BOOM! BOOM!
We're Miss Adventure and the Strangers
And it's gonna be a car crash.

I'm gonna get a reputation
For my sensational shows
It's the end of civilisation
Now everybody in the nation knows.

It is so not cool
To miss out on the boy / girl action
The only reason is it's pleasing
And we guarantee satisfaction!

Notes: Never really worked out the chords or recorded a demo. Flow of the third verse not good enough, but maybe could be made to work. Joe liked the idea. Maybe I should have another look at it.

Kick and Run
The way you play is absolutely rotten.
Your defeat will never be forgotten.
Your striker has been quieter than a dormouse,
and your midfield couldn't score inside a whore house!

Every bodies going flippin mental!
They say the we should play all continental,
we're going to stuff you and it won't be gentle,
just kick and run and "come on En-ger-land"

We are going to have the most possession,
you are going to have a big depression,
after giving you a football lesson,
we are going to have a wicked session!

We have got a brilliant formation
you are going to witness devastation
after we have taught you how to play son
we hope you like your long summer vacation.

It was our idea, we drink beer.
The beautiful game started HERE
4-4-2 we play route one!
Our strategy is called 'kick and run'

We dribble like our boots have got a magnet.
The cup will soon be in our trophy cabinet.
The referee is blind or out of his mind
but the English like to come from behind!

Ninety minutes gone and we're ahead now,
we're going to hoof the ball into row Z now,
your chance of winning really must be dead now
we're going to take your mother back to bed now!

We've got the greatest team and I'm not lying.
Soon the opposition will be crying.
It's going to look as if we're barely trying,
when we kick and run and "come on En-ger-land"
Kick and run and "come on En-ger-land"

Verse: **Chorus:**
A E A D E A   D A D E

Joke song from when I was interested in football. I would post it before a big game.

Talking to Yourself

There's ways of saying what you find dismaying
without baying like you've got a screw lose.
And there's ways of explaining why you are complaining
without doing my brain in with abuse.
But for what I heard
there is absolutely no excuse.
When you talk like that, you're just talking to yourself.

And there's ways of mooting what you are disputing
without sticking the boot in like that.
And there's ways of phrasing all the points you're raising
without blazing like an autocrat.
But when you rant and rave
and start speaking out of your hat,
get back in your cave, because you're talking to yourself.

Please stop behaving like a raving madman
that's craving to get his own way.
You can talk as effective without the invective
if your choice of words is a little more selective.

So try expressing what you find distressing
with more finessing of your prose and verse.
If you must speak out please don't freak out
or the veins in your neck might burst.
Try a little bit slower, volume lower,
and try thinking a little bit first?
Because when you talk like that
it's like Peter Cook without the genius,
like Samuel Beckett but more meaningless.
You're talking to yourself!

Verse:
D G F# F A (x2)
G G# A
D F A
D A C

Middle:
G D
G G# A

End:
D F A (x3)
D A D

Notes: My dad left me a ranty message on voicemail; so this was my counterattack. Thankfully I don't think he ever heard this song. It was pretty spiteful of me to write it - the sort of viciousness that sometimes mars Dylan's work. For all the wit it's a bit of an embarrassment now my dad has gone, and I realise what a great man he was, and how much he sacrificed for me. I was a bit of a snob towards him which I regret. At one point we were asked what the Chandeliers sounded like and Joe said: *"Polite Punk"* and I thought 'Of course – that's exactly what we are'.

Lives of the Rich and Famous
I'm like… "Oh my God…its AMAZING!…It's gonna be the next big thing…"
…Until the hot successes become the excesses of the beast within…

Lives of the rich and famous
draw idiots to their doom,
and the fools to the fame are the moths to the flame
there's nothing that it can't consume.
I so want to know what they're going to do next,
the magazine is coming out soon!
The marriage is on…it's off…it's on….it's off
"honey hold the honeymoon"

Parties of the rich and famous,
I would love to be a fly on the wall
to know what they said or did in the bed
before the decline and fall,
when everyone was staring at what they were wearing
before we stopped caring at all.
The marriage is on…it's off…it's on….it's off
….but the wedding dress would look so cool!

Trials of the rich and famous,
the only way to go is down.
The journalists are laughing, someone's photographing
an upstart after your crown
and if you stumble you'd better be humble
because it will be all over town.
The marriage is on…its off…the editors scoff…
rumour is they've *'been around'*

Life is a bitch for the poor poor rich as the promise of it all burns out.
You try to bankroll it, but no one can control how it turns out…

I could do with a little more cash right now
so I didn't have to work as hard,
and I could do with a little more cachet too
so I'm held in a high regard.
Then I could be free as Jay Gatsby!
and have more fame than Citizen Kane!
and gorge myself on unlimited wealth!
…till I'm exposed in all of my shame…
The marriage is…BACK ON…(but it wont last long)
They've been seeing someone all along!
SHAME ON THEM … never shame on us
for the lives of the rich and famous.

Intro:
Dm G C F
Dm G G#

Verse
C Dm C
Em G
Dm Em Am Dm G
Dm Em Am Dm G
C Dm Em F
Dm G

Middle section same chords as intro.

Last verse:
C Dm C
Em G
Dm Em Am Dm G
Dm Em Am (x3)
Dm G
C Dm Em F (x3)
Dm G C
G C

Notes: I was in the 24 hour Tesco at the top of Loampit Hill (by the College Café) and there were some celebrity gossip magazines. One headline said "CHERYL – THE MARRIAGE IS OFF!" next to it there was another magazine with the headline "KATIE – THE MARRIAGE IS BACK ON!". Never managed to fix the 'cachet' line.

Wake Up

Wake up, wake up,
a new day has begun,
a new dawn has come unto our skies.

The night was dark and long,
the starlight all but gone.
But now it's time to open up your eyes.

Let every colour shine,
let the future seize it's time
in the morning when the sunlight starts to break.
The shadows slowly dwindled,
the camp fire's been rekindled
and we have risen up and are awake!

Good morning friend to you,
let's check our diaries through,
what's on your list of things to do today?

We lived in fear and shame,
we dared not speak our name
and the horrors of our nightmares laid us low,
but now the daylight streams
but we've still got our dreams
and now were going to let our beauty show.

Music:
A C#m D A D A E
A C#m D A D A E
C#m D C#m D
A C#m D E
A C#m D A D E A

Notes: A precursor to my Brexit work. A cry for democratic uprising and a new society. I wrote a great melody for the words '*horrors*' and '*morning*' but wasn't good enough at singing to get it across; which is a real pisser as it's hooks that I'm missing.

Stop Pretending

we should be together
it should be forever
come rain or shine
let's pass the time
getting along whatever

and we should not be parted
tears should not be started
at the end of the day
when we're old and grey
let's not be broken hearted

there'll be no happy ending
unless we stop pretending
because when all's said and done
you've got to love someone
and you're good enough for me
so if I'm good enough for you
let's weather every storm together
all of our lives through.

Verse:
E B F#m
E B F#m
C#m E A E
C#m E B

Chorus:
F#m E (x3)
B
C#m E (x3)
B

Notes. I would walk around cafes in Brockley at the weekends, mulling things over on the walk. Although almost every line is a cliché it packs a musical thrill that maybe isn't apparent on the page. Has never bombed live either with the Chandeliers or acoustic. When I asked Vicky to marry me, I knelt down, and as I put the ring on her finger said: *"We should be together, it should be forever, come rain or shine lets pass the time getting along whatever"*.

Captain of the Ship

I am the captain of this ship
and my ship is very ship shape
with the safety of the vessel
and the passengers at stake.
My attention never wanders,
my standards never slip
because I am the captain
of a ship shape ship.

Though we may set sail
in a howling gale
I check each dial on the deck
and every last detail.
The sea fills me with terror
there is no room for error
so I keep a ship shape ship
until the hour we prevail.

The mighty waves are crashing
the icy winds are lashing,
we've got to pull together
when the lightning bolts are flashing.
The crew are treated fairly
spoils divided squarely,
because we won't have a prayer
lest we're ship shape and Bristol fashion.

I scan the constellation
and plot my navigation
sometimes I go by hunches
sometimes by calculation
until I see the seaside
and my family at the quayside
and at last we are together
and I've reached my destination.

Chords:
A C#m A Bm
A C#m E C#m
D E C#m Bm
A C#m A Bm A
A C#m A Bm
A C#m E C#m
D E F#m Bm
A C#m A Bm
Bm C#m D C#m
Bm F#m Bm E
D A D A
D C#m Bm E
A C#m A Bm
A C#m E C#m
D E F#m Bm
A C#m A Bm A

Notes: Definitely finished 2012 because I posted it on the same evening Team GB got loads of medals at the Olympics. Originally a comedy song but I shepherded it to seriousness. Superficially a children's song but fundamentally about adulthood. Always a great set opener. Maybe my best song.

Creature of Habit

Today is a normal day,
I got dressed in the normal way,
put on the same old suit
and commuted by the usual route,
carrying the same old case
I sat in my usual place.

Today is a normal day,
unexceptional in every way,
leafed through international news
taking note of the columnist's views,
said '*good morning*' to everyone,
and I looked through the work to be done…

I check my email
I check my email
I check my email and take a tea break
and then I check the female, top and tail
to be sure everything is ship shape.
And then it's back to my desk where everyone's 'stressed'
some THING'S cropped up…I might have guessed…
so I do what's due just to pay my way
because today is a normal day.

It's like yesterday but later on
I account for the hours that have gone.
File papers alphabetically,
It's probably how tomorrow will be.
And I need to work a little bit late
to be sure I have everything straight.

I check my email
I check my email
I check my email to see what they say.
Maybe someone somewhere that I once met
has written some THING on the internet!
And once I've clicked my mouse its back to the house
where I lay me down and drift away
into the same old dream of what might have been
because today is a normal day.

Notes: A poem I never got round to setting to music. Which is a shame as *"check my emails"* would have been a hook that would have stuck in the mind. Performed it at a spoken word night in Brighton - audience unimpressed with admission of lecherousness. There were several wasted years when I was just treading water at architecture offices. I told Johnny-Ray that my biggest regret was wasted time. Stupidly, I live as if I have more time than I really do.

We Came From the Seas

(bloop bloop)

We came from the seas.
We climbed from the trees,
and it was so neat – we stood on two feet
looked at the stars and scratched our fleas…
We made us some tools,
laid down a few rules
about how to behave, then we walked from the cave
where we'd painted on the walls…

A few centuries later
things could not be greater.
We made civilisation, declared a new nation
Then we took us a vacation
From appalling barbarity
to enlightenment clarity;
from the swamp to pomp and circumstance
rationality!

I attend to my grooming.
Progress is consuming.
I heard somebody say there's a crash on the way
and disaster is looming…HA!
The opera's divine my dear,
the ballet is sublime my dear,
but let's me and you take a trip to the zoo
this time my dear…

And so as we strolled,
what did we behold?
But such funny creatures…peculiar features
my – how we have evolved!
They have no civility.
They have no nobility,
they just mindlessly breed,
should they not be freed from their captivity?

What astonishing things we've done!
What problems we've overcome
since the day we made our way from the seas…

… So why the shadows? …
… still the shadows …
in the corners of my mind?
… those maddening saddening echoes
of what I thought was far behind …

We came from the seas.
We climbed from the trees.
We crawled from the pit
on our hands and knees.

I am an amphibian.
I am a mammal,
the Green Man, a pagan…
…an animal

We made us a fire.
We built an empire.
We worshipped false gods,
and the buildings got higher…

We mapped the constellations,
made all of the animals tame,
did endless calculations,
and gave everything a name.

But I just want to swing among the trees,
and sit and scratch my fleas,
and dive back into the seas…
…from whence we came.

(bloop bloop)

Intro:
B F# B F# B A# B
(X2)

Pt 1 Verse
B C#m7 D#m7 C#m7 F#
D#m7 E D#m7 E
C#m7 F#

Middle Section
D#m7 E D#m7 E
C#m7 F# B
C#m D#m E D#m
C#m D#m E F#

Punk Chorus:
G F#m Bm F#m (x4)

Punk Verse:
Bm G#m (x4)
End:
A Bm

Notes: A pretty huge achievement. The Chandeliers played it really well, but still I would love to hear it done by some band like Led Zep, the Beatles or Queen. I was shocked later to read that President Kennedy had made a speech that almost matched the last line word for word. (Remarks at the Dinner for the America's Cup Crews, September 14 1962) The line where I sing "*I am an amphibian*" is possibly the greatest Chandeliers moment. Just like my dad I can't lead or follow. I put a great band together and led them nowhere. I could have surrounded myself with second-rate people who I could blame for my failure, but instead surrounded myself with people I respected, who could do stuff I couldn't. I would bring them compositions and they would tell me how everything should be played. I got a lot of stuff wrong, but that part I got right.

Cheerio

Bye bye, cheerio,
its time I have to go.
Ta-ta, ta-ra.
Toodle-pip. Au revoir.

Since it all begun we've had such fun
with thrills and spills on the way.
It's been a hoot but time to scoot
we've got to call it a day.

Till we meet again auf wiedersehen,
what's done no tongue can tell.
It's been splendid but now its ended
take care and fare thee well.

We can't stay together here forever
hoping that things never change.
The moments gone we must move on
so till next time all the best sunshine.

Bye bye. Cheerio,
its time I have to go.
It begins with: "hi"
but must end with: "bye bye"
bye bye
bye bye
bye bye
bye bye

Intro	Verse (x2)	Last Verse
B B A# B B A# B	B F# E F# B (x2)	B F# E F# B
B B A# B B	D#m B (x3)	B F# E D#m B
C#m D#m E	E F#	D#m B (x4)

Notes: I once worked with someone called Blaise Kay who was a lovely character. He said *"cheerio"* and it struck me what a nice word it was. Any songwriter will tell you that you always have to be on the lookout for songs. I clustered a lot of *'goodbye'* type words together for this one. Clustering is a technique I often use. For the guitar intro I wanted something similar to *"You're Wandering Now"*. After the Chandeliers split I managed to persuade Milla to record it with me round her house with the dictaphone. I had the dictaphone switched to the ambient rather than the compressor mics which is why it sounds even more amateurish than it should. I sneakily arranged the singing parts so that Milla would have the last word on the album as I struggle with goodbyes. It's a nice ending. We parted friends. I miss them.

Making Hay

You've got to take your chances
in business and romances,
because you could wait forever
for the perfect circumstances.
When opportunity calls
be first out of the stalls,
it's no time to wait in line
playing by the rules.

You've got to make hay while the sun shines
or else prepare for sorrow,
because hey…if you don't make hay today…
what if the sun don't shine tomorrow?
Seize these opportunities
because life is all about…
…timing…
you'll have stacks of hay stacks
if you make them when it's shining!

You've got to make hay while the sun shines
or else prepare for sorrow,
because hey…if you don't make hay today…
what if the sun don't shine tomorrow?
And you're gonna feel real sore
if there's no bails in your store,
so if its sunny today…and you don't make hay…
then that will be…THE LAST STRAW!

Intro:
G# A A# B
A# A G#
C#m D#m F
E D#m E D#m
C#m D#m

Chorus:
B C#m B (x2)
B G#m C#m D#m
E D#m (x3)
C#m D#m B

Notes: Has the unorthodox structure and pace of *'It Began With A Smile'* but much more playable. Very easy for my sort of voice to sing. I've played it live numerous times and it never tanks. I would love to hear it done by a female vocalist with boogie-woogie piano, upright bass and a drummer using brushes.

Tomorrow Will Be Wonderful

Tomorrow will be wonderful when all of our cares are gone,
just get today out of the way and bring tomorrow on.
There are problems here and problems now,
but they will all be gone somehow,
and there will be just you and me
happy for eternity.

Chords:
A F#m C#m A
Bm C#m D E
A F#m A Bm
C#m A D E A

Notes: Mentally I always lump this together with '*It Began With A Smile*'. I made a collage video in which, over one day, from morning to bed time each word of the song is spoken by someone else. Again, mocking the idea that "*Everything you never did would have been perfect*". (My Life at Grey Gardens). Circa 2012.

I Hate Everything

There must be a shit conspiracy
perpetrated by all society,
to ensure that my life is an mindless chore,
everyone is having fun…except me!

The new stuff's shit the old stuff's past it
so I hate everything
I HATE EVERYTHING

It's not going in
I'm not listening
and if I listened I wouldn't care
it's just a meaningless nightmare
…so I hate everything…
I HATE EVERYTHING

They don't get what they do deserve
or they do get what they don't deserve
or they're too straight or they're a perv
…so I hate everyone…
I HATE EVERYONE

My political position:
the government is shit…and so is the opposition
the big parties are malevolent
the small ones are irrelevant
…I hate them all…
I HATE THEM ALL

It's not fair – while everybody frolics
I put up with pointless bollocks all day long…
pain pain pain pain pain
pain pain pain pain pain
…I know the answer … it starts with a BOMB!

Tomorrow will be like today
but just a little bit more grey
we're going to all die anyway
because pretty soon a big meteor
will end all life on Earth for sure
but so what? life is just a bore!
…and I hate everything…
I HATE EVERYTHING
(and I hate the ending too)

Intro:
C Em Dm C
Dm Em Dm C (x2)
Em Dm C

Verse:
Am C Dm

Middle:
Em Am Dm G
Em Am Dm Em

Notes: More self-mocking. Played it live (acoustic) about 4 times and it always went down well. Reminds me of dad saying: "*I hate everyone – it's quicker*".

True Love Express

All aboard True Love Express,
destination happiness,
calling at Elation Station
via Sweet Infatuation.

Boarding now for Love Express
departing station Loneliness.
Have your tickets at the ready
soon we will be going steady.

People wave goodbye to you,
the platform disappears from view,
the journey starts the train departs
and strangers say: "how do you do?"

Let it lead where hearts are freed
but think of others on your carriage,
hold on tight as you alight,
don't block the aisles with your baggage!

My my how the world flies by
and no return tickets back
We're riding till the siding
so be sure you're on the right track.

So it's all aboard True Love Express
destination happiness
calling at Elation Station
via Sweet Infatuation.

Verse:
D Em D Em
Bm D Bm Em

Chorus:
A Em Bm D
A Em Bm A

Notes: Written when I was having a happy holiday with Vicky in Boscastle, Cornwall. Now the idea of going on holiday without children seems odd. I wish I had more children earlier so I could spend more time with them, but that's my fault for wasting years being an indecisive tosser. With *'Captain of the Ship'* we see a 'children's song' that is actually about adulthood. This song is similarly uneasy – an upbeat ditty about love but with a sense of foreboding hanging over it, due to the enormity of the decisions we must make.

Don't be a Cunt

I sometimes think: "why is life so shit?"
When I look at the situation.
Then you rock up with some cock-up
and vwalla! I have an explanation!

So...please...don't be a cunt all your life,
please get it into your thick head,
I recommend you suspend
Conducting yourself like a dick head.

Maybe try using your brain,
It's starting to get depressing.
People would be happier if you was less crappier,
frankly it's unprepossessing.

The world is already full of cunts
it doesn't need anymore.
I've got a great idea. I'm giving you a steer
what the world needs now is...
LESS CUNTS HERE!

So might I suggest you give it a rest
because it's getting on my tits.
It needn't be all trouble and strife
if you stopped being a cunt all your life!

Chorus and intro:
F C (x3)
F F#m G
G F

Verse:
C F F# G C (x2)

Notes: A nasty vicious attack on my dad. At the time he had been acting like an idiot and had lost me £100k on a disastrous property venture in Herne Bay that will forever live in infamy. But now putting this book together eleven years later, he has just died of lung cancer and I realise what he gave me was beyond measure. There were about six times in my life when I declared war, 99% of them I subsequently regretted; maybe Brexit is the only exception. Thankfully I don't think he ever heard the song. He died knowing that I loved him.

Witchcraft

Well my car had broken down in a dodgy part of town
but I wasn't really fearing till I stumbled to a clearing.
The music there was rocking but the scenes were truly shocking…
it seemed I'd wandered into some groovy horror movie!

I'm not sure…but I suspect it was…witchcraft…witchcraft…

Well it was Halloween and I had never been somewhere so creepy!
There were zombies black cats and vampire bats it was freaky!
Cobwebs on the candlesticks, and weird supernatural chicks…
performing witchcraft…witchcraft…

There were druids drinking fluids that possessed the soul of everyone who tasted
and like a fool I drank the potion which affected my emotion – I was wasted!
Then I saw her in that vestibule dress, and she cast a spell of lustfulness…
It was witchcraft…witchcraft…

No man could have ignored her as she beckoned me towards her
I was helpless and totally consumed!
I was trying to resist her, but I couldn't so I kissed her
now I'm doomed DOOMED DOOOOOMMMMEEDDDD!!!

Now we rave hard in the grave yard doing lewd voodoo to woo you
its so frightful!
She's got tricks you wont believe tucked up her wizards sleeve
which are delightful!

It's a slaughter on the alter doing things we shouldn't ought to
A temptation situation with no salvation!
Its witchcraft…witchcraft…

Intro:
Am C Em (x3)
Dm D#m Em

Chorus:
Am C Em (x2)

Verse:
Am C Em (x4)
Dm D#m Em (x2)

Middle:
Dm Am C
Dm D#m Em

Notes: A story similar to the Rocky Horror Picture Show, I honestly hadn't thought of the similarity with 'Spooky' by Andy Williams till I heard it many years later. This song used to go down great and was un-droppable from the set. But the last few times I played it, it bombed so it's currently mothballed. The interesting thing here is the video. I saw a kiwi guy doing a puppet show with a skeleton called 'bones' on London's Southbank so I booked him for the video. (Jonathan Acorn of www.acornproductions.co.nz) £50 per hour but he was worth it! A brilliant film maker called Richard Carter-Hounslow filmed it. I made the set and we filmed the puppet a few times with different backgrounds. Then Rich said it was good as a video but needed one more idea. So I got some pictures of witches held their mouths with a bit of coat hanger and filmed it with my phone. Then another old friend Julian Tranquille edited the video for free which was amazing as he has edited James Bond stuff!

It Began With A Smile

It began with a smile.
It began with a look,
one tiny little moment is all it took.
It began with a feeling
a hand reached out
and any doubt was by the bye
in the twinkling of an eye.
Once upon a time
two people met somewhere,
and it began with a smile
and carried on from there…

Chords:
G# A (repeat)
A# B
C#m Em D#m
D C# D
C#m D Em
D C#m D E
A C#m A C#m
D E A
A G# A

Notes: At the time I felt this was a breakthrough with a medley of unique sections. I only played it live a couple of times. It went down well, but it's very difficult to play live. I don't think I've ever properly recorded it which is odd. We are back to Louis Kahn again and his famous poem about beginnings.

Take Care

Take good care of yourself
you are somebody's treasure.
Take good care of your health
your wellbeing is beyond measure.

It is insanity to say it is vanity
to have a little self respect
and if you're well read you'll know Shakespeare said:
"Self love is not so vile a sin as self neglect"

So when trouble is near don't be cavalier
discretion is the better part of valour.
When people are warring don't stick your oar in
you'll end up in Valhalla!

The people that care for you can't always be there for you
so I say a prayer for you every day,
because I would be sad if I heard that you had
not kept yourself out of harm's way.

Intro:
C Am C B C

Verse:
C Am C B C Am C C#
D Bm D C# D Bm D D#
C Am C Em
C Am Em

End:
C B C

Notes: not much to say about this. It would be nice if some pharmaceutical / wellness giant offered me loads of money to use it for their loathsome propaganda. I like that way the tune shifts in semitones to make it different to my other songs.

God Save the Queen

GOD SAVE THE QUEEN!
…she's nice in the extreme!…

She smiles and waves, she waves and smiles.
The best British leader by a million miles,
she's got a house with a moat and a massive boat,
it's the last British thing that can actually float!

Our monarch's the dog's bollocks
Why hasn't she got a statue?
Liz is the biz, Liz is the biz,
and she's got a well bling hat too!

Every year it costs just 70p
for the whole entertaining family.
And I wouldn't mind paying a little bit more
to be reigned on by her daughter-in-law.

Our monarch's the dog's bollocks,
it's why I am in a lather
Liz is the biz, Liz is the biz
She whacks battle ships with cava!

Some disagree and many scoff
but she's the only leader that's made us better off,
she puts up with cronies, political phonies
and boring opening ceremonies.

Our monarch's the dog's bollocks!
It cannot be disputed
Liz is the biz, Liz is the biz
She's had comparatively few people executed!
She's had comparatively few people executed!

Chords:
F C B (x2)
F C G C (repeat)

Notes: Silly song that went down great live. But inconveniently she died depriving me of a potential hit. Anyway this must have been circa 2013 because back then I saw the Windsors as part of our culture that should be protected from trendy modernisers. But then Brexit came along, the Windsors deserted us, and my opinion of them inverted. Whenever I see the newspapers now it is obvious we are being groomed to submit to some shit we didn't vote for, be it the royals, EU, Islam, plutocracy or mass immigration. Now I just file the Windsors under: *'rich, unelected and powerful'*. Why would mediocre people want a better system when they have prospered under a bad one?

Money and Beautiful Women

Money and beautiful women
Go together like cheating and winning
There's an attraction
There's an attraction
An electromagnetic chain reaction
Whereby the pretty girl in the party dress
And the rich and the powerful coalesce
Till the money's gone and the girls move on
And I'm left wondering what I've done wrong.

Politics and corruption
Go together like greed and destruction
There's an attraction
There's an attraction
An electromagnetic chain reaction
Whereby perfection gets state protection
Nobody is allowed to question
The vision's crushed, It's a busted flush
And I'm left wondering *'who can you trust?'*

Notes: Begun circa 2012 and finished 2024. I never got round to writing music for this one. Interesting how the chorus / hook is a third of the way through the verse. I felt it was quite dark for how I felt at the time.

Don't Worry About It

Some people get all stressed about
stuff they get depressed about
which makes them really vex about
what they should care less about.
Bothering is taxing
so I live by the maxim
there's less heart attacks in
maximum chillaxing!

I daaaaanwarrrryabaaaaa
(repeat this 4 times or else it will be wrong)

I do not exert myself
coz I don't want to hurt myself.
Why all of the urgency?
its not national emergency
Instead of getting uptight
cool down by two Fahrenheit,
drop the chore, do less more
chill real hard tonight...

and daaaanwarrrryabaaaaaaa

So take it easy dadio
things are not that bad-io
instead of getting mad HEY YO
stop being so sad y'know?
When things get problematical
don't just get fanatical
instead of doing that it's cool
to take a stress sabbatical...

And daaaanwarrryabaaaaa

Tune:
A A A A A B A E E E G G A

Notes: Rap that I did with a little keyboard on my shoulder. Mimicking the Schooly D photo with the boom box. This won me a couple of spoken word slams. Those were halcyon days at Bang Said the Gun with Rob Auton and the rest of the Bang Gang. I dressed up all comedy B-Boy. Sasha Jones said: *"Is that a tea cosy on your head?"* I replied *"Yes, but I'm wearing it in an urban way"*. At one point I emailed it to Blade and suggested we could record it together, but I think it was too silly for him.

The Night is Young

Good evening ladies and gents, it is my pleasure to welcome you
Without any further ado, to our program of entertainments.

It's 'hello' time. It's 'good to go' time. It's dress up top to toe time…
It's 'how d'ya do?' time, it's 'what's new?' time. Now there's no time like show time!

When the audience have expectations, and performers end their preparations,
To delight, excite and stimulate tonight for the amusements of our patrons.

The lives we lead are dull indeed, with boring chores and mouths to feed
So we seek something better at this theatre that our hearts and our minds be freed.

The night is young, there are songs to be sung
There are toes to be tapped, there are hands to be clapped,
There are stories to be told, scenes to unfold,
Drums to be rolled and jokes to be cracked.

So nice to meetcha! nice to greet ya! We've got a line-up booked to treat ya!
Its curtain up time, its lights out time, its shake it all about time!

The day's works done, the show's begun, so I'd like to welcome everyone
Its in your place time, its smile on your face time
When the day is old and the night is young!

Intro:
Gm F D# Dm Gm

Verse:
Gm F#m Gm
Gm F#m Gm
Cm Bm Cm
Gm F D# Dm Gm

Chorus:
Cm Gm A#
Cm C#m Dm

Middle:
D# Cm Dm A# (x3)
D# Cm Dm

Notes: I wanted something to open the show like '*Cabaret*' by Lisa Minelli or Sergent Peppers. Lots of my songs are either '*hello*' songs or '*goodbye*' songs. And with every album I tried to arrange the songs into a narrative like Sergent Peppers with a beginning, a series of rooms and a conclusion. Hellos are easier than goodbyes.

Until We Meet Again

Until we meet again,
till days are sweet again,
though it may be sometime
keep me in your heart
and I'll keep you in mine.

Till sun shines through again,
and skies are blue again,
long goodbyes upset me,
just please do not forget me
till I'm with you again.

Chords:
A C#m D
A C#m D
Bm C#m D C#m
Bm E
A C#m D
A C#m D
Bm C#m D C#m
D E A

Notes: Decent and no mistakes but maybe a poor man's *'Love or Money'*. Songs are so difficult I always just want them finished, which is maybe why mine are so short.

Same Shit. Different Day

I gave the DJ my promo
He said I sing worse than Yoko Ono
and maybe I should copy Bono
then I thought "Oh No!"
Same shit, different day
Same shit, different day
The calendar has changed a lot
Other stuff has not.

The leaders talk about poverty
They're very good at oratory
But the more they spend on equality
the poorer the majority.
Same shit, different day
Same shit, different day
the planetary alignment is dissimilar
Outlook – broadly familiar.

Sub-optimal mode – consistent
Dull situation – persistent
Prospect of fun – distant
Chance of a good laugh – non existent
Same shit, different day
Same shit, different day
The times have changed significantly
Other stuff, doesn't look much different to me.

Music:
G C D (played several times)

Notes: Just re reading this now it's better than I remember. A bit of a memory challenge to play live, but maybe I should try it in the set again – if anyone ever gives me a gig!

Fun Without Trouble

I want a beer that won't go flat, make me hungover or get me fat
I want fun, but without the trouble
I want the slide without the climb, the loot without the crime
I want fun, but without the trouble
I don't want a fancy job, just the fancy salary
The tasty food but not the calories
And to be like Kurt Cobain but without the fatality
I want fun, but without the trouble.

I want an outfit that is cool but completely practical
Cos I want fun but without the trouble
The face-lift without the surgery, the acquittal without the perjury
I want fun but without the trouble
I want to be a fitter person but without all the exertion
Play a cracking gig without any rehearsing
And if I have to choose I never lose and end up cursing
I just want fun, but without the trouble

I want every door half open, every 'what if' to be spoken
I want fun but without the trouble
To be together but apart, with every girl that crossed my heart
I want fun but without the trouble
To drift in endless dreams of party time distractions
Have a laugh and go down every path to new attractions
And to be exempt from any consequences of my actions
I want fun but without the trouble.

Notes: I never got round to setting this to music, but it won a few slams as a spoken word piece. Inverts the normal dynamic trick by getting quieter and more intimate towards the end.

In the Summertime

In the summertime
Everything is free and easy
And the world's a sight of such delight
It never fails to please me
I'm getting hot under the collar
Now the sun's come out again
And I'd bet my last dollar
When you're hot, you're the same

In the summertime
Suddenly there's more skin showing
Gents perspire, skirts get higher
No one looks where they're going
Last month we was snowed in
Now the air-con's overloading
And till its cooler clothes are smaller
And thermometers are exploding!

Love is in the air, its everywhere
So every care seems lighter
The world generally feels righter
When the weather's brighter

In the summertime
I put on my sunglasses
To be apart from this at the heart of this
And observe the world that passes
So till the sun is sinking
I'll get another drink in
And watch the ladies parading by
And wonder what they're thinking.

Verse:
Dm C Dm A Dm (x2)

Bridge:
Gm Dm A Dm
Gm Dm A

Chorus:
C Am Gm (x3)
Dm G

Notes: Written early 2014. I think it's a classic song. The second verse is perfection, but the third verse isn't as good and it's a bit long, so the last time I played it live I stopped after the first chorus. I attempted over 140 recordings before I got one that was ok. On the Tascam album its sounds different to the other songs because it's the only song I recorded in the kitchen.

Partied Out

Try to get my head around it
But only found its unresolved
Try to put my finger on it
But everything is so involved
It was a blast but it's the past, I need a taxi fast
I'm partied out
I'm partied out

Just holding it together
But everybody's getting uptight
Yeah we could split together
But I can't get my shit together tonight
It was a feast I was a beast, but now I need a priest
I'm partied out
Partied out

I can't stand it
To bail out now is distressing
But hanging with the freaks
Will equal several weeks
As a party casualty convalescing.
Im partied out.

I've got to make my mind up
Or wind up undone by excess
When all the shots are lined up
It's 'no tomorrow' and the rest is a mess.
It's time to end the session
Write my diary confession
I'm partied out
Partied out

Chords.
Standard Blues 1, 4, 5 in Minor 7s.

Notes: We had just moved to Brighton in 2014 a few days after Johnny was born and I played a comedy gig. One of the improv comedians said: *'I'm partied out'* and it stuck in my mind. The beginning of the verses came when I was at CZWG trying to get my head around some complex building problem. Had a lot of trouble trying to finish the third verse. I didn't play it live till early 2024 at *'Acoustic at the Constant Service'*.

Life is Short

Why can't we be happy when the sun still shines?
Must just dismay play on our minds?
Before the government makes happiness a crime
Let's smile while there's time.

Life is short, let's have fun
Now the evening is young
The future's only just begun
So let's love and love and love and love and love

Now the cares of today
Are far far away
Let's only work at how to play
And love and love and love and love and love

Sorrow is for tomorrow
Despair for somewhere else
But now I'm here with someone dear
So why not smile and hold them near?

While there's light in our eyes
And joy in our cries
And stars above us in the skies
Let's love and love and love and love and love
Let's love and love and love and love and love

Intro:
A E F#m C#m
D Bm C#m F#m
D Bm C#m A
F#m Bm C#m

V1:
A F#m Bm E
A F#m C#m
D C#m Bm A E

V2:
A F#m Bm E
A F#m C#m
D C#m Bm E A

Middle:
F#m C#m D A
D A D A
D C#m Bm E

V3:
A F#m Bm E
A F#m C#m
D C#m Bm E A
D C#m Bm E A

Notes: One day on the train coming home from Farringdon to Brighton I wondered if anything anyone ever said could have made a difference, and I felt the only words that might were *'life is short'*. I wrote the song without the intro. Then I read a poem by Philip Larkin about a hedgehog (or maybe it was lawnmower) it finished with the words *'while there is time'*. I thought this was a devastating phrase and that I should put it in a song. But rather than write a whole new song I just added an appendage intro to this one. The melody for the first line of the intro isn't very original - it's from a song called *'Spread a Little Happiness'*. Quite extreme how it is played, flipping from acapella to instrumental all the way through - that was the real development here.

OMFG

It was a normal day, going about my way
When quite unexpectedly
A sight of absolute delight
Presented itself to me.
My eyeballs popped, my jaw bone dropped,
I can't believe what I just copped,
And I'm not a guy whose easily shocked, but…
OMFG

Well I've been around and I've seen some things
That I never thought I'd see,
That you only expect with a special effect
You get when it's on TV
Quick double take, no mistake
I'm scared the internet might break!
My ghast was flabbered so I just blabbered
OMFG!

Well I'm not naïve but goodness knows
What I could do with one of those
So I swallowed and I hollered:
"THERE SHE BLOWS"
OMFG!

Chords:
A E
E A
A Am7 D Dm
A C# D
D E A
(Repeat)
C#m Bm
A C#m D
D E A

Notes: Not much to say here. Just started with the phrase and built the most audacious song I could manage around that. Carful and without obvious errors.

She Lives in Dreams

An ideal woman in a picture caught my eye,
and though it's said that cameras never lie
it briefly cast a spell, made me stop and dwell
on the many stories pictures tell...

She lives in dreams, in sunlight movie scenes
laughs in photographs adorning magazines.
There is a light, camera and action,
the make up's right, she's the attraction.

Attired tastefully, she enters gracefully
her way disarming, her manner charming
in each location, each situation,
she's quite delightful in conversation.

Her eyes look up and then look back again
its always spring when she's smiling
in summer breeze, in autumn leaves...
she wraps up warm in winters freeze.

I wonder if it is all it seems...
and I wonder what her half smile means...
if she remembers me, I hope it's tenderly
because she lives in dreams.

Chords:
Dm Em C
Em Dm
Dm F Em
Dm G
F Em Dm C
Dm Em F Em
F Em Dm C
Dm Em F G
Dm F Em Am
Dm F Em
F Em
C F Am G
F Em Dm C
Dm Em F G C
F G C (x2)

Notes: Maybe my masterpiece. Musically I wanted to do something like *'Love's Melody'* by Django Reinhardt and Steffan Grapelli. I am completely in control here. I set the scene, develop descriptively, list the seasons in the correct order and conclude with the big reveal. Maybe the chord structure isn't compelling enough to call it perfection but the syllables flow like water. Possibly Byron's *'She Walks in Beauty'* was an influence. Too subtle to play live.

You Don't Need God to be Good

You don't need God to be good
You don't need God to be good
You don't need revelation to show consideration
You don't need God to be good

It's all about doing what you'd like other people to do
Unless that involves other people spanking you
Whilst wearing rubber masks, tickling where you poo
Sometimes atheists do that too.
But you don't need God to be good
You don't need God to be good
You don't need a scripture to put you in the picture
You don't need God to be good

It began with a bang then the world then man
Then a myth took hold it was someone's plan
And that became the repository
Of every excuse and fantasy
There's no supreme being that's all-seeing
Who's going to judge and then do me in
It's a scam, a hoax taught by dodgy blokes
And were blasphemous for disagreeing
The human condition, our disposition
Comes from natural intuition
Not a war on reason where questions are treason
And it's a sin to think or listen

You don't need God to be good
You don't need God to be good
There's one rule – be reasonable
You don't need God to be good

But if you want to chop heads off and blow people sky high
First you'd better clear it with the big guy
And kit yourself out with a religious alibi
But you don't need God to be good

Verse:
A E F#m E
D A
A E A

Ending:
D A D E A

Notes: After writing this I wondered if I had (subconsciously) pinched the tune from somewhere. Then I realised that, of course, I had lifted it from Bach's *'Air on a G String'*. So I had plagiarised it from the most religious composer that had ever lived - thank God for that! You will be astonished to read that after I played it live, I was not struck down by lightning.

For Love of Money

Time weights heavy on my heart
though birds sing and it is sunny.
When you're happy time is fast, when you're sad the moments last.
You can't get peace for love or money.

The path has many twists and turns
in search of a pleasant destination,
and I can't find peace of mind for love or money,
but I live in hope, not expectation.

Chords:
D Bm G Em
G Em A D

Notes: At a site meeting in Kidbrooke the building manager said that such and such could not be obtained *'for love or money'* and I wondered what could really not be obtained for that. Joe produced a really good recording of it for the 'Create Beauty' EP.

Car

Why don't you love me like you love your car?
Just because your car goes places,
Just because your car takes you out round town,
Just because your car doesn't let you down.
Before you bought it I never thought it
Would change our relationship's basis,
But I note a tendency to devote a
Lot more time to your motor.

Why don't you love me like you love your car?
Just because it's got nice hi-fi,
Just because it's got some light that bleeps,
Just because it's got reclining seats.
I try to stay cool, but your vehicle
Is the end of the road for our marriage,
So pet me like when you met me, and let me
Park it in your garage!

Oh baby you – you <u>DRIVE</u> me crazy!
And I want to feel the same type of thrill
You get from your automobile!

Verse:
A E Ab A
D Bm D Bm
E C#m E C#m
D C#m Bm E
A F#m A C#m
C Bm A

Chorus:
C#m Bm
F#m Bm F#m C#m
C#m D E A

Notes: The '*you drive me crazy*' bit came first. I wanted a chorus hook beginning with a long high note like '*Just a Gigolo*'. Works well with my voice, the end of the second verse always gets a laugh.

Home Sweet Home

Home sweet home
Wherever I may roam
I yearn to be returning to
The place where we have grown
Round the final bend
At the journeys end
Where people who are dear to me
Are near to me again

As I step inside
The place where I reside
It's nice to see my family
With their arms open wide
Here's where I belong
How the time has flown
And we embrace, there is no place
Like home sweet home.

Chords:
A C#m F#m
Bm A E
C#m F#m C#m F#m
Bm E
C#m A C# D
D C#m Bm E
A C#m F#m
Bm A E
C#m F#m C#m F#m
Bm E
C#m A C# D
D C#m
Bm E A
Bm E A

Notes: Written on train journeys from work (in Farringdon) to home (in Brighton). My dad said it made him cry. A great conclusion to the Tascam album. Originally envisioned as a type of football song like *'Abide With Me'*. I would love to record it with a Welsh choir and a colliery brass band. Like *'Captain of the Ship'* and *'True Love Express'*, this is what I call a 'contradiction song' superficially it sounds very sad but actually it's about overwhelming happiness. So we see the shift from longing to happiness here and now.

Don't send messages when you're drunk

Don't send messages when you're drunk
Don't send messages when you're drunk
Don't send messages when you're drunk
Because you'll get the reply when you're sober.

Chords:
E A B E (x2)

Notes: Another note to self. Always fun live. After which I say: *'That's my social action track for the night'* which I copied from John Peel who said that after playing *'Masturbation Made A Mess Out Of Me'* by DQE. I'm going through a DQE phase again now, Grace Braun is great.

Hooray for Cabaret

We're in the entertainment business
This is the job that I do
That's why today, I came here to say
Hip hooray for cabaret.

We work in the services sector
We serve your vices well
That's why it's swell to get up and yell
Hooray for cabaret.

The only 'no no' is a no show
Boring is the only sin
So if you just walked in wondering;
"What is this?" Allow me to confirm
It's show business!

It's your duty to shake that booty
'Cos every lady here's a beauty
Don't vegetate, get fruity!
Hooray for cabaret.
(It's what we do)
Hooray for cabaret!

Notes: Another attempt to write a 'hello' opener type song similar to Sgt Peppers or Cabaret by Lisa Minelli. First two verses are decent but then it runs out of steam. I've never played it live.

Young Again

I want to be young again
I want to have fun again
And to do things that piss off everyone again
I want to be free free free
Shout out "me me me"
And not to have to bother with my family

I want to restore my cool
I want to go on the pull
And do things that are highly irresponsible
I want to take trips again
Kiss tender lips again
Insane delights just at my fingertips again

But time can't be undone
An old man can't be young
The past can't last forever
However it begun
So I just live for my children
And though sometimes I could kill them
I hope they live so long they long to be young.
I hope they live so long they long to be young.

Chords:
C Am Em F F Em Dm G x 2
Em Am Em Am
Dm G
Em Am Em Am
Dm Em C

Notes: I was going to work at CZWG in Farringdon. On the train journey (from Brighton) I had just been looking out of the window. I got off the train and started walking to work with all the people. By the time I had walked 50 meters I had the first few lines, so I stopped and wrote them down. Again, mocking individualism. End flips beginning. Must have been about 2015?

Mr. Sunshine

Mr. Sunshine, when I wake up in the morning
and another day is dawning, and I open up my eyes
I hear birds sing so take a look out the window
Everything's so simply lovely when you rise.

Mr. Sunshine, you make everybody warmer
so the flora and the fauna start to blossom in the park
and I step out in such a beautiful morning
there's no doubting I'll be happy till it's dark.

Until its dark I'm lost in wonder at the breezes and the thunder
and the rainbows that present themselves to me.
All the world is pure perfection laid out for my predilection
I got bored of all the sorrow and look forward to tomorrow.

Mr. Sunshine, when I get a little older,
and it feels a little colder, I'll simply say
for the time we spent together, when I had no umbrella
thank you Mr. Sunshine for every day.

Music:
G# Fm Cm A#m C# C#m G#
C# C#m Cm F
C# Cm A#m Cm
G# Fm Cm A#m C# C#m G#
C# C#m Cm F
C# D# G#
Cm D#
C# A#m Cm G#
C# A#m Cm
G# Fm Cm A#m C# C#m A#m
C# C#m Cm F
A#m C# D# G#

Notes: I realised I needed an opener for the Tascam album. I remember Bridgette Bardot sang a song called Mr. Sun. I can't remember anything about her song. I should go and re-listen to it now. But I thought it would be nice to write something a bit Pagan. Around 2015 I became an atheist. I had been very Christian in my 40s. In the 90s I had been talking to Nick Toyas and Kirsten Lyle at a party and Kirsten had observed that the Velvet Underground, Beatles and Beach Boys basically did religious music, whereas Led Zep may have sung about love but ultimately made war music. Public Enemy did conflict music, Schooly D was a storyteller, ditto Jarvis Cocker. Pixies – Torment. Bowie – alter ego. Morrisey – shyness etc. Most work is about one pretty simple theme. I conflated this and for the next 15 years assumed that the spiritual generated the meaningful rather than visa verse. My path to atheism was laughably predicable. My Brexit work got me studying Tom Paine (Deist) then Chris Hitchens, then Sam Harris then Bertrand Russell. Every year someone else changes my life. One year it was Andrew Sullivan, one year Kant, one year Schopenhauer, Hume, Rousseau etc. I did a Nietzsche phase when I was about 19, but generally I tackled the big boys after I was 45. I've never played this song live. I'm rambling. Anyway, not among my best songs but the important point is … I hadn't simply grown bored of the idea that profound work must be dark and personal, I had become hostile towards it.

Little Dreams

Each little cry, each little sigh
There was just love and you and I
How could we know how it would go
The night we said our first '*Hello*'?

Chords:
C Dm Em Am F Dm F Dm Em
C Dm Em Am F Dm F Dm Em C
Dm F Em C Dm Em F G
C Dm Em Am F Em F Em Dm
C Dm Em Am F Dm F Dm Em C

Notes: Good work. Set the scene, develop with description, rhyme 4 multi-syllable words and finish with the greatest final word of any song. Technically I'm in full control here, I don't have anything to say about the content.

Wasting Time

When we are at play
As we pass the day
As precious little moments slip away
Now I've done my filing
And we're happy and smiling
And I spend a while in
Your company this way

It's a silly game
Play it all the same
We climb and slide and climb and slide again
And the swings don't go nowhere
But neither of us really care
On the roundabout is where
Happiness is plain.

Castles in the skies
You look in my eyes
What's meaningless is meaningful
I realise
When we're wasting time we're not wasting time.
When we're wasting time we're not wasting time.

V1 and V2:   **V3:**
F# G   F# G
G# Am   G# Am
Bm G   Bm
Em D   Em C G
Bm Am   Em D G
C Bm Am D   Em D G

Notes: Another song about the greatest happiness – the unconditional love of family life. I was playing with Johnny at the playground in Brighton on the swings and slides, and he was smiling. It must be horrible being like the Rolling Stones - old men playing young men's music. As nature changes me, I write differently. I had depression all my life till I became a family man.

She Only Blew My Mind

She said '*hi*' so did I
Light was low, we danced slow
But at the end of the night when it was time to go
She only blew my mind.

She said '*it's late*', I said '*yeah*'
Got my coat - she's not there!
So I got a night bus home it wasn't fair
She only blew my mind

Now I've got to get a hold of myself.
Sometimes it gets so hard.
Just my luck, I said '*give me a call*'
Now my head is so messed up.

There was a chance at the dance
In a night of romance
But I just couldn't get into her pants.
She only blew my mind.

Verse:
Am7 Dm7
Am7 Dm7
Em7 Am7 Em7 Am7
Dm7 Em7

Middle:
Em7 Dm7 Am7
Dm7
Em7

Notes: Comedy song based on the double meaning of the word 'blow'. Parody of 'R&B'. I've only played it live once. I think it went quite well but can't remember.

You and Me

There may not always be a twinkle in my eye.
There may not always be stars up in the sky.
Everyday concerns seem to come and go,
We watch our children grow. everything must flow

There may not always be bills I have to pay.
There may not always be jobs to do today.
There may be a time when I'm not on a mission,
Fretting or regretting. Everything's transition.

There may not always be trouble on my mind.
An ache within my heart or doubts of any kind.
But as long as there is love, as long as there are lovers,
There will be you and me and a melody.

V1 and V2:
A C#m D A
A C#m D E
(D A) x 3
D E

V3:
A C#m D A
A C#m D E
D A D A
A F# E A

Notes: I was listening to *'Give me a little more time'* by Gabrielle and I was thinking about how wonderful it was. I imagined myself to be a music journalist writing a review of the song. What could I say about it? What praise would be high enough? I decided the only thing I could say about the song was: "*As long as there is love, and as long as there are lovers, there will be this song.*" That got me thinking again. "*As long as there is love, and as long as there are lovers*" was a great lyric. What would there be? You and me. And what? A melody. That was the punchline written. Then I just clustered a list of transient things together for the first two verses.

Ones and Zeros

There's a lot of ones and zeros
They must be extremely small
Such a lot of ones and zeros
I wonder how they count them all?
It would take me quite some time
Imagine if they were in a line
It would stretch from here to the stratosphere
There must be tonnes of ones and nones!

There's a lot of ones and zeros
whizzing all about the place
faster and faster, vaster and vaster
and if they crash it's disaster!
If all of the sums of ones and nones
just disappeared without a trace
Imagine the look on Bill Gates' face!
There must be tonnes of ones and nones!

Music:
D A
A D
G D A D
G D
A G A D
A G A D

Notes: Sometimes the computer freezes and you get the 'blue circle of death' spinning in the centre of the screen. It's frustrating but then I think how it long it would take me to do what I just asked the computer to do.

How Much Do You Need?

How much do you need? What more could you wish for?
At what point do you say: "*There is nothing I would swap this for!*"
"*I have an excess, would settle for less,
I wouldn't swap what I've got under duress*".

How sweet the delight, how strong the attraction.
But when do you say: "*Today, It's satisfaction.
"How simply divine! I'm drawing a line
All things considered I figured this'll do fine*".

Because you've got what I want,
So if I've got what you need,
And we put what I want with what you need,
That would be very good indeed.

Verse:
A F#m C#m Bm
C#m Bm
D C#m Bm C#m

End:
D Bm C#m A
A C#m D
C#m A

Notes: Another song mocking myself. One could go on wanting more forever. Began with the first line.

(I want a man that's) Good With His Hands.

Some men are handsome, some have degrees
From prestigious universities
The type I like is not like any of these.
Good men address practicalities.

I want a man that's good with his hands.
I like a guy who gives things a try.
I need someone who can get the job done.
I like a man that's good with his hands.

Don't want a suitor who taps a computer.
Don't want a show-off who would just go off
It's cool if he's tall but overall
I want a man who's good with his hands.

Someone unique who can deal with my leak.
A real catch to sort my damp patch.
A sensation of the service penetration.
I want a man that's good with his hands.

A want a lover who don't love another.
I want a friend who'll be there till the end.
So I figured, all things considered
I want a man who's good with his hands.

Chords
A C#m Bm A
D C#m
D C#m Bm A
A C#m Bm

Notes: I had the idea whilst doing carpentry. At that point the Chandeliers were emailing one another, and it was one of the songs I sent round. I would love for us to record a version with Milla singing as she has such a great voice. Joe memorably said the fourth verse was *"maybe a double entendre too far"*. Joe recorded a demo and sent it around to the Chandeliers. This remains the only time the best version of one of my songs was recorded by someone else. I played it live a couple of times and (as Joe predicted) the 4th verse bombed. One time at Cabaret Lab I opened with it whilst wearing a silly wig, establishing conclusively that I am the worst drag act in Brighton. But anyway, here it is in its entirety so others can include / omit as they see fit. Melodically compelling, five syllable rhymes for fun, it works well live.

There's Always Washing Up

Sometimes pigs fly and politicians don't lie.
Sometimes there is a blue moon in the sky.
But there is one fact that's true till I die,
There's always washing up.

Sometimes I have fun, my football teams won.
Sometimes there is an eclipse of the sun.
But there is one job that's never quite done,
There's always washing up.

I do the washing up, make a cup of tea.
Nice tasty drink but inevitably,
The cup in the sink is down to me.
There's always washing up.

Sorry to ramble but here's a new angle,
To get rich quick, I've got a hot tip
Buy lots of shares in Proctor and Gamble.
There's always washing up.

1st Verse:
G Am G Am
C Bm Am G
C D

2nd & 3rd Verse
G Am G Am
C Bm Am G
C G

Middle:
C Bm Am G
D E
G Am Bm C
C D

Notes: Actually I quite like doing the washing up. I made the sink and draining board at our house in Kemp Street and it's nice to watch gravity drain the crockery. When I do the washing up it's a time when I am doing stuff for the family so I feel I'm being useful, but I also get to listen to some Youtube thing about Bitcoin (if I'm being lazy) or philosophy (if I'm pushing myself). Vicky says I take ages doing the washing up so I can listen to my shows. Once I've finished, I go upstairs and help putting the children to bed which is lovely. I am happy.

My Dream Came True

My dream came true and we were lovers
I put you first before all others,
And when we touched under the covers
My dream came true.

Our secret words were softly spoken,
It was as if we were awoken,
Our hearts and eyes completely open
My dream came true.

We made our way through life together,
And swore we'd stay in love forever,
I could not be more happy ever,
My dream came true.

Optional verse:
We made our way many a mile,
Giving our best all of the while,
I held your hand and saw you smile,
My dream came true.

Chords:
C G Dm Am
F C Dm
C F C

Notes: Not sure what I feel about this one. I started out writing 'My dream never came true' as it was such a powerful phrase - my idea was it would be a dark vengeful song - but then decided to invert it. Recorded a very badly sung version for bandcamp. Maybe I will listen to it in a few years and knock it into shape.

'Girlfriend'

My girlfriend's a superfreak
Her equipment is unique
Her genitals rewrite the rules
My girlfriend's got two testicles!

The sex was like nothing before,
My mouth was full, my bum was sore
I said "MORE! MORE! MORE! MORE!"
She said: *"take that you dirty whore"*.

But if 'she' is a he or 'he' is a she
That's confusing as can be
I expected a socket a little love pocket
But it was a fallacy!

I wondered if it was a sin
Her balls were bouncing off my chin
How can a bloke not be a bloke
When he's got a nob to stroke?

Chords:
D A D G D A D

Notes: Another humdinger smacked out. I haven't played this one live yet but Joe assures me that when I do I will be booed off. I don't care, I'm not going to scorn climate denial but placate gender denial.

Head Honcho

I'm the head honcho
I'm the CEO
I'm the dirt expert
It's a TKO
From the DOB
To the RIP
Mister Twister
Number one MC

I'm the rhymer, stanza designer,
Best in show, syllables flow
Forget all the rest no contest,
Probably guessed they're a one-liner.
Jackpot if you like it or not.
Oh what a lot of lyrics I got
Crem de la crem, ten out of ten
That's first verse, chorus again.

Hum dinger, non-beginner,
Serial winner but average singer
Dim the light and rock all night and
Keep it tight and lady excite and
Guess who it is when they say 'gee whiz'?
Gets on the mic and do the biz.
I give you three guesses, getting warmer,
Turn the corner, what's in the box? I played a stormer.

More in the tank, premier rank
Article don, rivals blank
Amazing phrasing no two ways
How it plays out I blaze a trail and phase out
You and nothing new crew to the unknown zone
I write all night, they write ring tones.
High ambition. I'm on a mission.
Rivals listen it's a demolition.

Chorus:
(Am Dm) x 2

Verse:
Am Dm Am
Em F Dm C Am
Am Em F

Notes: Considering that I grew up with Hip Hop and have written heaps of rhymes it's astonishing I've done so little Rap stuff, so I set myself a challenge to see if I could do it. I realised actual talking would sound silly with my voice and that I would have to put tones to each syllable. So although it's a bit of an oxymoron, I ended up with a rap / song! Another oddity is that when I tend not to write choruses, but the moment I had a go at Hip Hop (which traditionally doesn't need choruses) I suddenly ended up with more choruses than verses!

We Are Together

I was alone,
Nobody to care for
I was young,
Hurting everyone myself as well
But you have to take a stand someday,
And stick with something come what may.
Try to make it better, not walk away.

And so we met,
It wasn't always easy.
I was upset,
There were times I had enough.
What if it had not worked out?
If we had given in to doubt?
What's the most important thing life's about?

But we stuck with it through thick and thin,
Forgiveness is the greatest thing.
Now whatever misfortune this life may bring …
(oh baby now)

We – we are together.
There isn't just a you and me, separately.
A single note is not a harmony.
We – we are together.
There isn't just a me and you,
One and one isn't two,
But a unity of love our whole lives through.

Tune:
C D Em D C D Bm Bm
Bm open Am Am open Am Am open
C Bm Em

Verse: G C Am D x2
Bridge: C G C G C D
Chorus: G C G C G C D G x 2

Notes: I wanted to write a male / female duet like *'Islands in a Stream'* but with a feel like *'I found loving'* by the Fatback Band. Structurally it's like a wave that builds up, similar to *'Live Together'*. For the independent tune I wanted a procession like Mendelsohn's *'Entrance of the Queen of Sheeba'* that gets played at weddings. Maybe some of the lyrics had a similar feel to *'I'm a Lady'*. The idea is the man sings the first verse, the woman sings the second, and both sing the end.

Double Denim

I'm rocking double denim
I'm in double denim heaven
My jeans are blue, my shirt is too
Everyone's jealous but what can they do?

I am so elated
It's co-ordinated
Feast your eyes, you can surmise
I've got shares in Levis.

Chords:
G Am Bm
C Bm C Bm
Am D
G Am Bm
C Bm C Bm
Am D
G

Notes: Another hit off the old Handley production line. I finally managed to find a denim shirt that fitted and was well made. It was made by Pepe, not a top name but the stitching was perfect. Oh the triumph of sauntering around in my Pepe and matching Wranglers (I don't actually have any Levis). It's got a five-syllable rhyme like 'Weddings' and 'Little Dreams' and like 'Washing Up' and 'Ones and Zeros' it references a big company at the end. There's nothing to this songwriting lark.

Boy Meets Girl

Boy meets girl
It's a story old as any told
There's a time and a place, a look on the face
A glint in the eye, a word, a reply
There's new styles, but always smiles
There's new fashions, but always passions
In robes or rags, rubber or leather
For ever and ever and ever and ever
Humans want to be together
So, boy meets girl.

Girl meets boy
It is a universal rule
Every plant, every animal
Even those so small, you can't see them at all!
The birds and the fishes, each living thing misses
The touch that will fulfil their wishes
From mountain peak to ocean deep
Though each mating call's unique
It's the same song all along
Of boy meets girl. *
Boy meets girl.

Chords:
C Dm Em
F Em F Em
Dm G
F C F C
F Em Dm C
Dm Em
C Dm Em F
(* F G Am for 2nd last line)
F G C

Notes: Came together quickly. Begun early July 2025, with words and music finished by 9th July. Graham Lyle once told me his best songs tended to come together quickly. Hopefully that is a good omen. I will have to record it ASAP. It felt like a classic song so I made it two verses because White Christmas (Berlin) Summertime (Gershwin) and An Die Music (Schubert) are all two verses. Lots of words presented themselves so verses are longish, hopefully that made the chords less predictable. Clustered lyrics together so one verse is about history and the other is about geography.

The Sky is Blue

Lying on the grass, looking at the sky
Out of the corner of my eye
A gable, a branch a telephone cable
They'll still be there when I die
One day they will fall down too
But the sky will always be blue

Paddling in the sea, daughter and me
I smile at her, she smiles at me
Soon we will go home for tea
But waves will lap eternally
When we're gone they'll carry on
Breaking for some other someone
But the reason we hold hands and smile
Will still persist all of the while
As long as one thing is shared by two
As long as the sky is blue.

Notes: Staying round the in-laws in Forfar. (July 24) Before bed I had stupidly had two massive bits of Toblerone so I couldn't sleep till about four in the morning. Lay awake and planned out the basic material, then sneaked downstairs and jotted it in a Tesco magazine. Tore it out, folded it and put it in my shoe. It was a nice surprise the next day to look in my shoe and see the sleepless night hadn't been a complete waste. Moral: don't eat Toblerone before bed! Rhymes a bit conventional and monosyllabic. I think I have done this theme now, time to move on.

Food, Shelter You

It is elemental
Completely fundamental
What is most essential
Is being kind and gentle

Food, shelter you (x4)

Wherever life is leading
Don't want much exceeding
Housing, loving, feeding
Three things I am needing.

Food, shelter you (x4)

More than completely, very very sweetly
In the morning when my love greets me
We smile and we laugh and wander down the path
Hand in hand upon our journey.

Verse and chorus chords:
G, Am, Bm, Am, C, D, G, D x 2

Into and outro chords:
G, Open, Am, Open x2
G, Bm, C, Bm
C, Bm, Open, Am, Open, Em, Open
G, C, D, G

Notes: Many years ago (Circa 2010) I used to go to Farago poetry slams, run by a lovely guy called John Paul O'Neil. There was a great poet, a black guy, I can't remember his name, but he did a poem called 'Food Shelter You' which really cut through. He really stood out from all the hyperventilating ranters. Many years later (2024) I was listening to a lot of Reggae and thought I needed to write something of similar simplicity, so I took his line, turned it into a chorus and set about writing verses for it. I would love to know his name so I can credit him. Get in touch please!

Chemistry

I think we're gonna work it out
I think we're gonna work it out
Beyond a shadow of a doubt
This is what it's all about …

Chemistry then biology, it's physically about you and me.

We've experimented, the conclusion
Life was just confusion
Now it's terrific, so scientific
Theres going to be a fusion!

Chemistry then biology, it's physically about you and me.

My predilection is for affection
It's out of the question
Evolution is the solution
That's natural selection

Chemistry then biology, it's physically about you and me.

For every action there's a reaction
That's the satisfaction
Of forces that determine courses
That's what makes attraction.

Chemistry then biology, it's physically about you and me.

Intro:	**Chorus:**	**Verse:**
D A G (x3)	D Bm G A	D Bm G A (x2)
A G		D

Notes: I had the science idea knocking around for years, but it came together in a flurry mid November 2024. After the success of 'Boy Meets Girl' I wanted to do more impersonal objective stuff. I like to imagine people smiling.

Delivery Man

I love shopping on the internet
It's amazing all you can get
Pre-landfill, clothes that don't fit
Then look for a loan to pay for it.

They say that I'm a raver - a spender not a saver
I should modify my behaviour
But I can't stop picking items for clicking
Add to the basket – it's shipping!

My credit cards bust, but spending's a must
When I get the statement, I'll be concussed
I'll make Jeff Bezos richer than Elon Musk
The plan depends on Delivery Man

Delivery man delivery man
Get me the package as soon as you can
I'm looking out the window waiting for the van
The plan depends on Delivery Man

Knock knock ring ring. He's got my thing
I'm so excited what he's gonna bring!
Soon I'll be taking off the packaging
The plan depends on Delivery Man.

Rat-a-tat-tat. How about that!
Guess what landed on my welcome mat?
If it don't fit I'll just send it back
My plan depends on Delivery Man

Knock knock, how d'ya do? Package for you!
(you won't believe the traffic I've come through)
Sign on the line, See you next time
Because I'm the Delivery Man.

Chords:

1st Verse:
B, F#, B, D#m, E
E, B, E, F#, B

2nd Verse:
B, C#m, B, C#m
B, D#m, E, B

Typical Verse:
B, D#m, B, D#m, E, F#
B, D#m, E
E, B, E, F#, B

Whistle:
B, C#m, B, C#m
B, D#m, E, B

Notes: No prizes for guessing how this came about. I always imagined it being sung by a woman rather than me. Maybe I should have put more emphasis on the delivery man being the real object of the woman's desires. Stuck in a couple of extra verses that can be omitted if they make it too long. Fin January 2025

Enough

Alone in darkness I remember
Days of youth and love and happiness
Now it's gone everyone's moved on
Memory – the only thing that I possess

Looking at something in your eyes

Now all the moneys worthless
I'm richer and poorer than I've ever been
Thank God I gave myself completely
Thank you for loving me so sweetly

Looking at something in your eyes

The big stuff is the small stuff
Small stuff is the big stuff
I have loved and I have been loved
That is enough.

Tune and Outro:
D, D, D, C#m, Bm, Bm
C#m, C#m, C#m, Bm, F#m, F#m
Bm, Bm, Bm, A, E, E
C#m, C#m, C#m, Bm, A, A

1st & 2nd verse:
A, D, E, F#m, Bm, C#m
A, D, E, F#m, Bm, C#m
F#m, Bm, C#m, A

Notes: Stylistically a mash up between An Die Musik by Schubert and Coney Island Baby by Reed – two of my favourite songs. I'm haunted that I wasn't with my father when he died. I should have visited him the day before. It was a huge shock to get the call from the care home that he had suddenly gone. I thought I had more time. I tried to write about what we might think when we can't even write. Fin early Feb 25. Struggled with 2nd verse. When I die, like my dad, there probably won't be anyone there so I want them to know this.

Daddy is the Best

There is a gent who's really excellent
10 out of 10, one hundred percent.
He's so cool it's indisputable
Everyone is in agreement.

Daddy is the best guy ever
Daddy is the best guy ever
Daddy is the best guy ever
Everybody knows it's true

It is nice granny visiting
Kids are ok (when they don't sing)
Family are irritating
Mum's not bad – if you like that sort of thing – BUT

Daddy is the best guy ever
Daddy is the best guy ever
Daddy is the best guy ever
Everybody knows it's true

Verse:
F#, G#m, A#m, B, C#, Am
Chorus:
F#, G#m, A#m, B, C#, F#

Notes: Putting Iris to bed she came out with the chorus in a happy moment. I cobbled a couple of verses together to make it a song. Started just before we left Kemp Street January 2025. Finished early Feb.

Passing Through.

Back around 1996 I had been working on a building site with Marcus McDonnel (boxing referee and brother of Jim) and his workmate Frank. I had been drilling a hole and I burned out the drill which I felt bad about as it was an expensive one. I was told that with a drill you have to go in and out repeatedly so that there aren't sustained periods of resistance. 'In and out'. The phrase stuck with me. Around 2010 I was going to poetry slams (Poetry Unplugged, Bang Said the Gun, Farago, Vapor Vox, Hammer and Tongue etc). As a songwriter, poetry slams were revelatory, and if you are a songwriter / rapper I urge you to give them a listen. So I started writing a poem, but whereas other people did intelligent stuff like writing various poems to see what worked, I decided to torture myself by writing more and more verses for a magnum opus poem that was virtually impossible to finish. I would drop this or that verse depending on the theme of the night and how much time I had been given.

Every day I earn my pay
commuting to where I start computing.
Drawings are amended, notes appended,
scheme revised list systematised.
So many numbers to check and inspect
till the job's signed off and they're all correct.
So for the regeneration of the nation
lots and lots of information
goes in and it comes out again
it goes in and it comes out again.

And at the end of the month my pay is credited,
thereafter it is direct debited
it goes in and it comes out again,
it goes in and it comes out again.

Then with my cash I go to the shop
then from the shop on to the bus stop
where I twiddle my thumbs until the bus comes
and I get on and I get off again.
I get on and I get off again.

From the bag to the fridge to the oven to the plate
to the fork to the mouth to the throat to the gut.
From the kitchen where the meal began to the bathroom to sit on the pan,
taking care not to forget a book to read and a cigarette.
I take a toke and I watch the smoke.
It goes in and it comes out again.
It goes in and it comes out again.

Caught in rain I can't complain
the garden's looking green again.
Yesterday it was forlorn...
Strange how quickly things transform.
Water is absorbed by roots
nourishing the little shoots
that grow the stems that grow the leaves
upon the trees that bear the fruits.
I pick a berry and inspect it
marvel how nature perfects it,
squeeze it just a little bit
juice squirts out, the skin is split.
On my shirt it's made a stain
and doesn't taste the same as rain,
the droplets now are sweet and red
that went in and came out again.
It went in and it came out again.

I see the girls in the new styles,
they're talking and I see their smiles.
Going to their things to do
they're walking and the sight beguiles.
It's fascinating and delighting the clothes that they go out at night in:
there's the sporty types the lady likes and the hippy chicks and the urban-ites...
so I appreciate the care they take in choosing what to wear
whatever the occasion or the weather
which combination goes well together?
Things with studs are in right now,
but flares aren't worth a light right now.
Young ones don't listen to their mums,
their pants are much too tight right now!
So ... things with studs are well regarded
but soon will be discarded,
they came in and they'll go out again.
They came in, and they'll go out again...

Less of the dizziness, down to business!
At a club and its in full swing
clear to your ear the beats deafening.
Everybody is rocking and the party's cool
so people get loose and more sociable.
Gotta rock gotta rock till the rhyming stops
every line I write has to be the tops,
so I come correct and you won't forget
how the text connects and I tick the box!

Nobody knew the chandelier swung like that
and it was even appealing when the ceiling cracked,
but there can be no ceiling to what needs revealing
look up, look up, look up, look up,
look up…to be a human being.
This is secular religion,
a beauty contest
a style war
a search for meaning.

I watch the DJ do his thing,
he takes records and makes them spin,
looks at the crowd then in the bag
and selects the next for mixing in.
A little more groovy, a little more groovy,
a little more hectic and more energetic,
till the groove it went into becomes a new song to sing to
and everyone else gets into the thing too.
His job is to select
and every choice he makes must be correct,
one false move and he'll kill the groove
so with utmost care he picks the set,
makes his choice in a timely fashion,
takes the record from the cover,
lines up the beats so they won't be clashing,
and fades from one tune to the other.
It comes in and it will go out again.
It comes in and it will go out again.

I try to think clear
I drink a beer.
You have got all sorts around here…
so much to do before I'm through,
I must write a book (maybe next year)
Then amid the din new thoughts begin
someone goes somewhere to do something
I watch the personalities and situations
and drift on in my contemplations…
Everybody here is looking for love
with secret thoughts and stolen looks
private wishes and longed for kisses
it's wonderful what all of this is,
for there's a truth that I see now
I swear I must never forget
but as the night becomes the day
the truth here now will drift away….

I must describe each last dimension
bestride all thought and comprehension
set the universe out in song and
paint each possible expression.
So I go through where the years have gone
and try to work out right from wrong,
and what I ought and what I oughtn't,
I'm trying to convey
I'm trying to relay
I'm trying to say…what is *most* important.
And it's clear the truth is near
to set out what all of this means,
but I'm always elsewhere never here
and the truth is lost somewhere in dreams…
and the moments gone, the worlds moved on
so I step from the throng into the john,
and I'm thinking as I hold my dick and see a pool of someone's sick:
"*It goes in and it comes to again*
It goes in and it comes out again"

Me and a girl, we were together,
we were young then, she was the only one then.
Love was blind so we touched instead
and thoughts wandered where fingers lead,
which affected her which affected me,
we gave and took simultaneously:
from the mouth to the ear to the mind to the hands
to the skin for the cycle to again begin.
And so I felt, and so she felt,
till the way we felt changed the way we felt,
till *her* reaction to *my* reaction was almost perfect satisfaction…
where beyond beyond beyond beyond
beyond all of the games and teasing
the only reason is that it's pleasing
and it goes in and it comes out again!
It goes in and it comes out … but then …

… nine months later I rushed to enter
an elevator at a medical centre,
then exited the elevator I'd entered
and made my way to the prenatal theatre.
I remember the gas and the injections
the forceps and midwife's inspections,
the breathing then the pushing
and some other things I will not mention.

And so the night's events unfurled
as from the womb into the room
a human dawn, a child born
the future came into the world.
One girl stopped crying and another started,
and I wasn't sure what I was supposed to do
I hugged the mum and cried: *"thank you thank you thank you!"*
She said: *"where is my baby?"*
And then we took what we had done
and the little life that we had begun
and the beginning (of the beginning) was fun!
… but it goes in and it comes out again …
it goes in and it comes out again.

But I'm being glib, it's not as neat as that,
things don't just suddenly change tack
one moment when the shutter clicks
one moment when the balance tips.
In time there are subtle transitions
we look, we see, we make revisions
and assume our new positions
in between the moments when
things enter and go out again.
For example, when all this is through
me and every one of you
will leave this place we came into,
because all of us have 'stuff' to do…
everyone is passing through…

We came in and we will go out again.
We came in and we will go out again.
We came in and we will go out again.

Haikus

Now for some haikus
they are very short poems
this is one of them.

What is a haiku?
It's seventeen syllables
five, seven then five

That's five syllables
then its seven syllables
then five syllables.

That was a haiku.
This is another haiku.
Here is another…

Haikus are easy
because they don't have to rhyme
and they're very short.

Haikus are great fun,
every now and again
I just knock one out!

Some poems are shit
but at least a shit haiku
won't test your patience.

The trouble with them
is by the time you get it
it's done and dusted.

That's enough haikus.
Everyone's bored of them now
Ok. Something else…

(alternatively)

That's enough haikus.
Everyone's bored of them now
Thank you and goodnight.

Momentarily
the future held so many
possibilities

Many were louder,
few were more memorable.
Wizard Of Skill – Peace!

It was exactly
how I hoped the day would end,
walking back with her.

Alcohol is great
I feel like a genius…
No one must read this!

I feel like a god
Alcohol is brilliant
I had forgotten…

The path not taken
is the repository
of your fantasies.

Rushing for the train
holding hands with her husband,
she didn't see me.

It's still unfinished…
Can you create anything
if you don't believe?

I lie here awake
planning out everything
that will never be.

It's not the drink that
messes you up, but going
to work the next day!

War has been declared,
so don't vote for anyone
without a peace plan.

I have decided
each of my Facebook updates
will be a Haiku!

What is the point in
reading anything unless
it might change your mind?

Being together
is learning to love something
that is only real.

I am currently
out of the office on leave
and don't give a crap.

Out of the office.
I am on annual leave
so you deal with it.

Dear Sir or Madam,
stop sending me this bullshit
Yours faithfully, Seb.

There's so much to do
hum drum technicalities…
We all waste our lives.

What is next to you?
Write about the here and now
to make it timeless.

There is no Heaven.
I'll go despairing at the
things I'll never see.

Preparing before
and tidying up the mess,
the job's half the job.

Standing on the deck
of a red Routemaster bus
is the finest thing.

It's only the guy
not doing any rowing
who can rock the boat.

Make yourself the best
and ask for the rewards
of being the best.

Life doesn't happen
at a convenient time
however you plan.

This haiku is wrong
because the last line's missing

The good thing about
this general election
is they will all lose.

I lie here awake,
Going through all the decisions
that led to this point.

We can only dream
in our reflective moments
of what might have been.

"Write when you are drunk
Edit when you are sober"
(Earnest Hemmingway)

Writing, like people
is the assemblage of
mundane elements.

What's it all about?
Knowing is the easy bit.
Think, and do good work.

In pictures there is
everything we imagine
but will never be.

Realpolitik
is just a middle-class phrase
for appeasing thugs.

You can never know
what the path you didn't take
would have lead you to.

The last time we met
we said to meet again soon.
It was like a dream.

You're not one person
but part of a family.
We are together.

Sebastian's dead.
You should have paid attention
back when it mattered.

I lie here awake
ruing what will never be
and what might have been.

The secret is that
there isn't any secret.
You just have to work.

There was a big bang
then on the ten-billionth day
Man created God.

CHICKS! FAME! and MONEY!
Everything you never did
Would have been perfect.

Mum waves me goodbye
Till we fade in the distance.
My daughter's the same.

What if they left now,
With everything unresolved
And goodbyes unsaid?

What you feel, we feel.
You are not just one person
You are part of us.

When you're sad, I'm sad.
We're not individuals,
We are together.

If you use twitter
To try to sell me something,
Sorry but, goodbye.

'*Hello*' is easy
But trying to say '*goodbye*'
Never feels complete.

'*Goodbye*' can't be true
Because if it was so good
Then why would we part?

Moments at parties
When people are so careless
And we really see.

I can't get to sleep
So I plan conversations
That will never be.

Spare me the lecture
Don't like the establishment?
Then don't vote for it.

Spare me the lecture.
You don't like terrorism?
Then don't buy petrol.

Spare me the lecture.
You don't like slavery?
Then don't pay for it.

Spare me the lecture.
Don't like conservatism?
Then try something new.

We only realize
how perfect life used to be
when something goes wrong.

Everybody wants
the government to get tough
with everyone else.

If you don't believe
in a meritocracy
stick with what you know

26 letters
3 colours and 10 numbers.
Mundane makes meaning.

I can't get to sleep.
But I'll be drifting away
When the alarm rings.

I was excited
to see I had an email
but it was from me.

Profound work is the
Thoughtful assemblage of
Mundane elements.

Check and double check
It is a constant struggle
Just to think clearly

The thing that I think
When I do not think at all
I know must be true.

I lie here awake
In my imperfect present
And remember you.

Stockholm syndrome is
When you indulge the people
You are fearful of.

Why do you suppose
The people at the top
Are not into change?

The establishment
Will always be against change
Out of self-interest.

We are born helpless
And we grow and help others
Till we die helpless.

In the show business
the only cardinal sin
is being boring.

A photo of you.
I know the meaning of life...
don't need the last line.

My wife is pregnant
Heaven is when we feel good
about the future.

There isn't a line
between hate speech and free speech.
They are the same thing.

I enjoy the work
Just as much as they enjoy
Paying the wages.

Your perfect system
Is a catastrophe but
You can't admit it.

You're in denial
About the shortcomings of
Your perfect system.

When did she decide?
When did the no become yes?
When did the tide turn?

There's too much to do.
When it seems overwhelming
Organise your work.

I read it again
Wondered what good it could do
And deleted it.

Where open debate
And fair criticism end,
Bad decisions start.

Your enemies want
You to be disorganised
Downcast and lazy.

When we're wasting time
In the playground together
We're not wasting time.

In my darkest hour
I will remember my love
Smiling at me.

Money in the hat
of the accordion man.
It's a fair exchange.

They might attack you
but the ones who don't speak out
are dead already.

As I lay dying
the last thing I say will be:
"*no further comment.*"

The people who yearn
for simple arcadia
just never grew up.

People who yearn for
a pastoral existence
are never happy.

In a sleepless night
You will remember someone
Who said "*I love you*"

The profound makes the
Spiritual important not
The other way round.

Don't show everything
Or they'll soon be bored of you.
Be mysterious.

Having a belief
Allows you to be more wrong
And less repentant.

If girls want to know
what boys really talk about,
it's your worst nightmare.

The time together
everything open but eyes
I never forgot.

Nothing can be done
about what has passed except
reinterpret it.

I am wide awake
In the middle of the night
Thinking about you.

Nothing's more profound
Than knowing one day you must
Say goodbye to them.

The true life is sweet
Because the sweetest pleasure
Is never tasted.

Curious that where
religions are the strongest
there is the most sin.

You think life is shit
Till it gets worse and then you
Look back with fondness.

I enjoy my job
About as much as my boss
Enjoys paying me.

Who has the best tunes?
God or the Devil? Neither.
Human beings do.

The greatest poems
are the ones we could never
put down on paper.

To enrich us all,
everyone should do something
that makes them poorer.

Fear, depression and
Worrying about whatnot
Don't solve anything.

The most important
Moments in your life are the
Hellos and goodbyes.

Now they're gone I would
Give anything to go back
To the bad old days.

Christianity
Didn't make morality
It's the opposite.

From morality
We get religion. it's not
The other way round.

Comedians are
The greatest philosophers
And vice-versa.

My sweetest darling
So long as I have my mind
You will have my heart.

She won't remember
But I remember her well
We met once briefly.

If belief had a
rational basis then you
Wouldn't need belief.

Significant things
Are assemblages of
Mundane elements.

Youth is when you are
Out of your mind until she
Is out of her mind.

Belief systems fail
The only ones that work are
Listening systems.

Adam Smith was a
Describer, whereas Karl Marx
Was an explainer.

If you do what you
believe in, then get ready
for disappointment.

Everybody knows
What everybody should do
Except themselves.

The human problem:
You can want what you don't have
But not what you do.

You can't define love
There are as many meanings
As there are lovers.

Belief is the PROBLEM
It's the act of having views
You can't justify.

Thank you for writing
I always look forward to
When our paths next cross.

What is a mind for?
It is to think, nothing else.
Not for believing.

Whatever you do
Don't do what you believe in
Reduce suffering!

Then they came for the
Cunts. And I did not speak out
For I was not one.

Animals become
Minerals that may become
Living things again.

I throw some money
Into the wishing well and
Wish for more money.

You can't be happy
Until you stop thinking about
Your own happiness.

Great art is not made
by the unlearned or learned
But by the learning.

For every action
There is an opposite and
Equal reaction.

Every time I fly
I make the solemn promise
Not to fly again.

Waves appear to move
But the water doesn't much
Just the energy.

Modernist sculpture.
I don't know what it's saying
But it sure means it!

Kant's God argument…
A proof not based on reason
is no proof at all!

Creationism
Does not explain how we are
Darwinism does.

How do we critique
The Critique of Pure Reason
except with reason?

'*Populism*' is
A swear word used by those who
Lost the argument.

One day there will be
a last time that we meet and
a final goodbye.

Having children means
No sleep, fun, time or money
It is wonderful.

Energy equals
Mass times the speed of light times
By itself again.

($E=MC$ Squared)

The last time we met
We talked about this and that
It was like a dream

E is MC Squared:
Mass times the speed of light squared
Equals energy.

The movement of waves:
Force moves horizontally
water vertically.

There is nothing more
Philosophical than to
be drunk and dancing.

I don't advocate
an answer. I advocate
A method – reason.

My darling children
May there forever be a
Twinkle in your eye.

Children intently
Do things that are meaningless
Just like the adults.

First ever haiku by Johnny-Ray Handley:

Today is rubbish
I don't even like today
I'm down in the dumps.

It's unbearable
It will all be forgotten
I can't sleep again.

Do you feel angry?
Every time I declared war
I regretted it.

Philosophers have
no sex or children, but ask
"what is happiness?"

Philosophers have
No sex or children but ask:
"What is the good life?"

My darling children
Somethings only become clear
With the passing time.

Everything you do
Should be for the benefit
Of everybody.

Everyone's life is
A great adventure if you
Tell the story right.

The blue dragonfly
Is a blur like happiness
These things come and go.

Some are better at
synthesising but nothing
is original.

All philosophers
are cursed to be forever
ignored or attacked.

The greatest meaning
is a connection between
two human beings.

Aristotle said:
"Excellence is a habit
We are what we do".

Be nice to your kids
because they are the ones who
read your diaries.

Forces move in lines
and also in waves unless
they are influenced.

Atoms contain force
but forces don't contain atoms
we are energy.

I am an atheist
I will be very scared when
the time comes to die

When life ends on earth
there will be many children
who will not grow old

Somewhere in the dark
a star will shine forever
just for you and me.

When you feel alone
you can bring me back to life
by reading my words

The embarrassing
rantings of my former self
publish everything!

If you don't like it
you're free to vote against it
except that you can't.

When farts aren't funny
you know your relationship
is in deep trouble

Children fuss over
the silliest little things
just like the adults.

All philosophies
taken to their conclusion
are insanity.

Heaven is a place
where we say all of the things
that we never said

The passage of time
with its countless memories
is unbearable.

If I had one wish
it would be for this old mind
in my young body.

Read my diaries
so you might get things right that
I kept getting wrong.

Blame was so easy
I was right and she was wrong
Now I blame myself.

We must say goodbye
To everyone forever
and be forgotten.

The joy of love and
the regret of anger are
both never ending.

Time to sleep.
My son is scared of the dark
He says: *'please don't go'*.

I walked with my friend
to where we took separate ways
meaning is mundane.

There are many loves
that have begun and ended
at the dragon bar.

When they are too old
or too young to understand
we say we love them,

Philosophy is
a silly career choice for
intellectuals.

Immanuel Kant
Never was so great a mind
So shit a writer.

The tap is dripping.
Could a tap drip forever
And never run dry?

We find ethical
reasons to do what is in
our self-interest

Plants are animals.
They just operate on a
different time scale.

All philosophies
taken to their extremes are
a total head fuck.

The important thing
is what you keep putting off.
(haiku for my kids)

My father is dead.
We argued about money
it seems silly now.

A happy life is
only having to worry
about little things.

Everybody knows
what everybody else should do,
but we are all trapped.

We see ugliness
in the here and now. Beauty
in the there and then.

My last words will be:
"*Before I go I just want
to check my email*"

When I persevered
I succeeded ... but failed
when I walked away.

I was looking for
my glasses, but realised
I was wearing them.

Haiku for Johnny
When you are alone
Walking home drunk late at night
You are not alone.

I thank the women
Who in saying '*no*' to me
Saved me from myself.

Some Jazz is so bad
only a white middle class
teacher could like it.

If you look for shit
You won't have to look too long
Before you find it.

Eroticism
is not in seeing it, but
in not seeing it.

Eroticism
is looking for something, but
never seeing it.

The good times are not
the times without sadness but
times you don't regret.

Unhappiness is
the pursuit of happiness
excluding all else.

Everything you get
(it's the curse of the rich man)
You must give away

Photobooth

It was his idea
He had been acting strangely
Money in the slot
(FLASH!)

He produced a ring
It is never the right time
"Will you marry me?"
(FLASH!)

She looked at the ring
She looked at the camera
She looked in his eyes
(FLASH!)

It was a gamble
"I'd be proud to be your wife"
Tenderly they kissed
(FLASH!)

(25.02.26)

Bits and Bobs

It only takes 30 seconds to use a cash machine – unless you're in front of me in the queue, in which case it takes a billion fucking centuries.

It's not the all-night drinking that messes you up – it's going to work the next day that does the real damage.

If you believe in religious freedom then you must also believe in people's freedom to not be religious.

Everything I make is a monument how to live.

It is a constant struggle to think clearly.

When is an apology not an apology? When it's a justification.

Life is just endless disappointment and misery.

People will only read a partisan essay if they've already made up their mind.

The future won't be how you expect.

No one is beyond temptation.

If you want to influence, be influenced.

I write and write, then at the end, I write the title.

Yes, I can multitask. For example, I can watch the TV and not give a fuck simultaneously!

You only have to buy a Mars bar to see how capitalism works, but you have to study at the LSE for ten years to learn how Marxism works.

What is real? What exists? Or what we think exists?

Thank goodness for the gays. If it wasn't for them no one would be having children in wedlock anymore!

The coolest people aren't cool.

Cole Porter wrote about simple things in a sophisticated way.
Irvin Berlin wrote about sophisticated things in a simple way.

The future of the world will depend on how you treat women.

No debate is unanimous. If it was it wouldn't be a debate.

Fuck happiness. Why do you think I worked all these years?
For happiness? No, I did it for a better tomorrow.

If you want to succeed, read.

If you write, write with all your heart, because this time will never come again.
(Dream 07.03.16)

Dad. Sometimes we hated one another, but we always loved one another.

A good song causes many tears.

I'm happy with my songs that make others cry.

     to spend this life on this path and the next life on every other path. No notion is more seductive than the idea that one may live one's life *and* the life that might have been.

Make a large number of small decisions with your mind
And a small number of big decisions with your heart.

Marry the right person at the wrong time.

Joanna Lumley – the face that launched a thousand wrists.

You can have what you want, but you can't want what you have.

Mathematics only has certainty only because the answer IS the question rephrased.
Where the answer is not the question, there is no certainty.
= & describes R synonyms

THE ANSWER IS NOT THE ANSWER. THE ANSWER IS THE PROCESS.

I've decided to start a group called '*Comedians Against Easily Offended Cunts*'

When you're angry, don't be angry, be organised.

Love is a time.

When you read my words you bring me back to life.

Nothing can be as good as what we imagine.

To get, give.

When you are young an hour is an age.
When you are old an age is an hour.

Poem for leaving card:
'May the journey be learn-y, earn-y and one day, return-y.'

Perfection is too short.

We are memories. To forget is to die.

I would rather be forgotten than remembered as a cunt.

Better to be hated for what I am, than loved for what I am not.

Revenge is self-harm.

No painter can make primary colours from secondary colours, but my geraniums can!

Forgiving others is easy. Forgiving myself is impossible.

"*One day*" = never.

The more simple the question, the more complex the answer.

Sensible things come and go.

Easily offended people can fuck off.

Apparently men who don't masturbate are more likely to get testicular cancer.
This PROVES that lying gives you cancer!

I was going to write a song called '*Procrastination*' but then I thought … well … er …

When I think of all the people who have loved, and all the people who will love, and all the things important to them that will be forgotten, it's overwhelming.

Me: What do you want to be when you grow up?
My daughter: Bigger.

It is more pleasurable to be good. For to be bad gives but a moments pleasure and endless regret.

When saying '*I love you*' is easy, when it's hard to *not* say it, say '*please marry me*'.

Why are the cleverest, the silliest communicators?

If it don't make sense, it won't make dollars.

Citizen Kane had everything. What did he want? Rosebud. Not because it gave him Kantian disinterested pleasure, but because it gave him interested pain. It was the most precious thing precisely because of the pain it brought. To have it was to possess the life he led as well as the life he didn't lead. It was the physical manifestation of everything that might have been.

We see ugliness here and now, and beauty there and then.

If you're looking for a reason, you've already found it.

If you look for shit, you don't have to look long.

You have good days, and you have bad years.

When you're pissed enough to see it, you're too pissed to write it down.

Where should the future be decided? Not within but between.

Every painting is a self-portrait.

Knowledge and belief are mutually exclusive and inversely proportional.

Work hard to make it look easy.

I'm such an artistic failure I will probably win the Turner Prize!

I got a mortgage the other day – it was like buying a cappuccino!

Truth is hard at the beginning, sweet at the end. (Ditto work)
Lies are sweet at the beginning, hard at the end. (Ditto laziness)

Here comes Mr. Cheeky
Here comes Mr. Cheeky
One of his shoes is squeaky
Mr Cheeky really should wise up
When he leaves the toilet, he forgets to do his flies up.
He thinks of silly faces and trips up on his laces
Wearing baggy trousers without a belt or braces.

(Never finished that one. Circa 1992)

Poem about how young people can struggle to come to terms with bereavement.
OMFG
URIP!
WTF?
No LOL!!!!

Weirdo

Weirdo - it's worse than I feared-o
It's not cool, you are abnormal
Your behaviour is not de rigueur.

(That's as far as I got with that one)

My dearest darling Johnny

They will tell you to be quiet
They will say everyone has rights except you
They will demand standards they can't meet themselves
They will say there is something wrong with you
That you're inferior mentally or physically
They will say there is no place for you
And that you're not a proper human being
But just remember you are my beautiful son
With a spark of life worth more than money
And whenever you smile
Somewhere in the infinite
I am smiling too.

(2024)

Song for Iona

This is an unfinished poem from around 2010. I think it eventually got rewritten to into 'Unknown Soldier' and 'Until We Meet Again'. It's odd that the most important people in my life are not necessarily the ones who obviously dominate the writing - but they are all there below the surface. Around 1994 I wrote a great poem for Iona in my sketchbook. I was on acid at the time. It must be in the attic somewhere.

When I'm not here to hold you near
Please say a prayer for me
When far away, all I ask is
Say a prayer for me

Remember me each time you
See the sunshine breaking through
And I will do the same thing too
And say a little prayer for you

When you say goodnight turn off the light
and say a prayer for me
I should have never gone away
I should be with you now today

There Aint No Santa Claus

From around 2005. John Dawson played me '*This Plane is Definitely Crashing*' by Modest Mouse and I tried writing something like that.

There aint no Santa Claus (he doesn't really exist)
There aint no toof fairy (they don't exist either)
NNNNNOOOOOOOOOOOO
There aint no Easter Bunny
(there's Easter and there's bunnies but no Easter Bunny what brings you a egg)

Mission: work hard, educate yourself, think ahead.

Johnny: Capitalism is flawed.
Teacher: What's the solution?
Johnny: Death.

If my songs need someone with a PHD to explain them, I've failed.

'What's Best … ?'

What's Best? is a game I invented with Patrick Lynch (Circa 1996?) It's very simple to play: below is a list of *'What's Bests'*, at the next soiree just start reading them out in any order you like. Feel free to dispute / vote / debate / digress or propose alternative *'what's bests'* as you go on … A memorable evening will ensue…

What's best … hose pipe or watering can?
What's best … belt or braces?
What's best …window boxes or allotments?
What's best … Les Paul or Fender?
What's best … lace-ups or slip-ons?
What's best … buttons or zips?
What's worse … being in a porn film that nobody watches or being in a film that everybody watches?
What's best … polo or V neck
What's best … spots or stripes?
What's best … russet or burgundy?
What's best … side burns or moustache?
What's best … drainpipes or gargoyles?
What's best … drainpipes or flares?
What's best … still or sparkling?
What's best … now or the good old days?
What's best … a life of fun plagued by guilt, or bored righteousness?
What's best … carrots or parsnips?
What's best … gas or electric?
What's best … opera or ballet?
What's best … tights or stockings?
What's scarier … zombies or vampires?
Who's best … Karl or Groucho?
Who's best … Lennin or Lennon?
ok, no more messing around (and this is the booglariser) Curtis Mayfield or Jimmy Cliff?
Who's best … Liza Minnelli or Judy Garland?
What's best … berries or blossom?
What's best … here or there?
What's best … necklace or ear rings?
What's the most anti-social…mass murder or daytime television?
Who's best … Chuck Berry or Little Richard?
Who's best … Buddy Holly or Little Richard?
Who's Best … Stevie Wonder or Marvin Gaye?
Who's best … RUN DMC or Public Enemy?
What's worst … overpopulation causing ecological catastrophe, or loads of people getting wiped out?
What's best … North America or South America?
What's best … chandeliers or candelabras?
Who's best … Frank Lloyd Wright or Louis Kahn?
What's worse … looking ridiculous and being oblivious to it, or looking ridiculous and being painfully aware of it?

What's worse ... dandruff or flatulence?
What's best ... magnolia or taupe?
What's best ... scratching or human beat box?
What's best ... wallpaper or paint?
What's best ... fitted carpets or rugs?
What looks sillier ... complying with health and safety procedure or being horribly mutilated?
Who's best ... Joe Meek or Phil Spector?
What's best ... guitars or keyboards?
Who's best ... Elvis or Frank Sinatra?
What's best ... Marlon Brando or Robert De Nero?
Who's best ... Matisse or Picasso?
Who's best ... Pete Sampras or Roger Federer?
What's best ... heals or flats?
What's best ... fanny pads or tampons?
What's best ... beginnings or endings?
What's best ... roller skates or BMX?
What's best ... tea or coffee?
Who's best ... Johnny Cash or Hank Williams?
What's best ... Grease or Cry Baby?
What's stupider ... screwing your boss or your employee?
What's best ... Chanel or Dior?
What's best ... scones or hot crossed buns?
What's best ... kipper or slim jim?
What's best ... Impressionism or Expressionism?
What's best ... waiting or walking?
What's best ... hat or haircut?
What's best ... traffic lights or belisha beacons?
What's best ... eaves or parapet?
What's best ... gambling or fighting?
Who is the most pointless ... a 'left-wing' politician that increases unemployment, or a 'right-wing' politician who increases spending?
What is the most tasteless ... vegetarian food or eating meat?
What's worse ... someone pleasures you but you find it degrading, or someone degrades you but you find it pleasurable?
What's best ... to be fashionable and wrong or unfashionable and right?
What's best ... to have existential doubts about something that's real, or absolute certainty in something that isn't?
What's best ... space or stuff?
What's best ... staff that show initiative or staff that do as they're told?
What's best ... tradition or progress?
What's best ... why or how?
What's best ... flawed reality or perfect fantasy?
What's best ... Spring or Autumn?
What's best ... sponges with scourers on the back or dish brushes?
Who's best ... us or them?
What's best ... Friday or Saturday?
Who's worse ... the leaders or the followers?

What's best ... humane mousetraps that don't work or inhumane ones that do?
What's worse ... deforestation or Sycamore trees?
What's best ... calculations or hunches?
What's best ... naive optimism or depressing realism?
What's best ... the past or the future?
What's best ... stick or twist?
What's best ... questions or answers?
What's best ... looking best in photos or in real life?
What's best ... nobody knowing you're a genius or no one knowing you're an idiot?
Who's best ... Humphrey Bogart or Clark Gable?
Who's best ... James Stewart or Carey Grant?
What's best ... getting paid or getting laid?
What was best ... the 19th Century or the 20th Century?
What's best ... being admired for your humble frugal lifestyle or being reviled for your grotesque affluence?
Who's best ... Divine or Leigh Bowery?
Who's most shit ... Phil Collins or Peter Gabriel?
Who's best ... Peter Sellars or Spike Milligan?
What's best ... Chinese food or Indian?
What's best ... plant pot or window box?
What's best ... in the thick of it or out on a limb?
What's best ... front or back?
What's best ... top or bottom?
What's best ... mild or mature?
What's best ... inside or outside?
What's best ... plants or animals?
What's best ... blood in your piss or piss in your blood?
What's best ... death or dishonour?
What's best... cheese or sweet?
What's best ... utensils or fingers?
What's best ... hairy or shaved?
What's best ... sharp stabbing pain or long dull ache?
What's best ... normal or strange?
What's best ... giving or receiving?
What's best ... knowing or not knowing?
Who's best ... Andy Warhol or Lou Reed?
What's best ... fluids entering or fluids leaving?
What's best ... words or pictures?
What's worse ... dying young or growing old?
What's best ... soft or crusty?
What's best ... flattering or not flattering?
What's best ... simple or sophisticated?
Who's best ... John Walters or Russ Meyer?
What's best ... cool or hot?
Who screws things up the most ... the conservatives or the radicals?
What's best ... Ghost Busters or Back to the Future?
What's best ... smooth or textured?
What's best ... letting it grow or letting it go?

What's best ... fitting in or not fitting in?
What's best ... looking or listening?
What's best ... logging off or logging out?
Who are the most tiresome ... the offensive or the offended?
What's best ... common sense or consistency?
What's worse ... being stared at or overlooked?
What's best ... The Man With Two Brains, or The Jerk?
What's best ... Mods or Rockers?
What's best ... youth or experience?
Who changes things ... the outsider or the insider?
What's best ... shaken or stirred?
What's best ... fork or spoon?
What's best ... mani or pedi?
Who most need to shut up ... those who can't *make* a joke or those who can't *take* a joke?
What's best ... ketchup or brown sauce?
What's best ... skinny or grande?
What's best ... in the pink or in the black?
What's worse ... green or yellow?
What's best ... mussels or winkles?
What's best ... Def Jam or Sugarhill?
What's best ... heroic failure or reviled winner?
Who are the most boring ... the ones that think dope should be legalised or the ones who don't?
What's best ... speed or stamina?
What's best ... popular music or unpopular music?
What's best ... standing up or sitting down?
What's best ... gaps or overlaps?
What's worse ... fresh air that's the wrong temperature or stale air that's the right temperature?
What's best ... plain living and high thinking or plain thinking and high living?
What's worse ... talking nonsense or listening to it?
What's best ... same or different?
What's worse ... silence or violence?
What's worse ... having everything to do or having nothing to do?
What's hardest ... knowing what you want or getting it?
What's best ... competence or enthusiasm?
What's best ... scattered all about or all in one place?
What's best ... bearing up or bearing down?
What's preferable ... grilled or roasted?
What's best ... power or principles?
What's best ... mother's ruin or wife beater?
What's best ... hearts or diamonds?
What's best ... looks or money?
What's worse ... mess upstairs or mess downstairs?
What's best ... contentment or the pursuit of happiness?
What's best ... rest or restlessness?
What's worse ... rubbish coming out of your mouth or rubbish going into it?
What's best ... cake or biscuit?

What's best ... thinking or not thinking?
What's best ... before or after?
What's worse ... private vice or ostentatious virtue?
What's best ... learning or teaching?
What's worse ... temptation or guilt?
What's worse ... being talked about or not being talked about?
What's best ... looking up or looking down?
What's best ... moderation or excess?
What's best ... a good reputation or a bad one?
What's best ... mystery or revelation?
What's best ... on the wagon or on the tiles?
What's scarier ... science without religion or religion without science?
What's best ... quality or quantity?
What's best ... being persuasive or having a massive gun?
What's best ... more responsibility or less?
What's best ... witty fool or foolish wit?
What's best ... with style or au naturel?
What's worse ... to rise by sin or to fall by virtue?
What's best ... reserved or available?
What's best ... liberty or conviction?
What's best ... being born great, achieving greatness or having greatness thrust upon you?
What's best ... camouflage or shiny boots and buttons?
What's best ... top down or bottom up?
What's best ... balls or aerosols?
What's best ... saving or scoring?
What's best ... nice to look at or nice to listen to?
Who's best ... T.E or D.H?
What's best ... grand or upright?
What's best ... graceful or disgraceful?
Who's best ... Frank or Nancy?
What's best ... rock or skate?
Who are the most pissed off ... the left or the right?
What's best ... nuts or bananas?
What's best ... leaning forward or leaning back?
What's most exhausting ... attending or declining?
What's best ... Panama or Derby?
What's best ... English or continental?
What's best ... plan or elevation?
Who's worse dressed ... cyclists or Colonel Gaddafi?
What's most interesting ... your phone or the rest of the world?
What's most boring ... discussing weight or skin colour?
What's worse ... impassioned rudeness or grudging apology?
What's worse ... an hour too soon or a minute too late?
What's worse... head in clouds or head in sand?
What's best ... lumping or splitting?
Who's best ... Phillip Larkin or Eric Morcombe?
What's best ... great country with shit leaders, or shit country with great leaders?
What's worse ... albatross round your neck or monkey on your back?

What's best ... right but repulsive or wrong but romantic?
What's worse ... violent minority or silent majority?
What's best ... ex or next?
What's best ... in or out?
What's best ... a man on a journey or a stranger comes to town?
What's best ... rice or noodles?
What's best ... bang or whimper?
What's worse ... boredom or stress?
Whose best ... Ferry or Eno?
What's best ... theory or practice?
What's worse ... gnawing anxiety or shock horror?
What's best ... associate or partner?
Who's best ... Howlin' Wolf or Captain Beefheart?
What's best ...Songs of Travel or Winterreise?
What's best ... saloon or salon?
What hurts most ... before the end or after?
What's best ... a bird in the hand or two in the bush?
What's best ... the devil or the deep blue sea?
What's best ... things that last a long time or things that last a short time?
What matters ... who you meet or when you meet?
What is ... being or becoming?
What's best ... body or soul?
What's best ... comedy or tragedy?

Very Approximate Timeline

Born 21.10.68.
1977 – Met Nick.
Circa 1985 - Joined Starlite Rockerz (Martin Spiers, Joel Vigil, Chris Robinson, Tony Riordan and later Valentine Mason)
Circa 1986-7 - DJ with Blade. Met Claudette.
1988 - Iona born.
1989 - Moved to Gwent to study 3D design.
1991 - Transferred to architecture at Southbank.
1992 - Lived in Lyon met Paddy.
1993 – Moved to Solon Road. Happy days with Jezza, Justin Franey, Stuart Franey and Simon French. Took Acid.
Circa - 1994 Left Southbank. Lived in Hales buildings Elephant & Castle.
Circa 1995 - Met Colette. Moved to Limes Grove.
Circa 1996 Started at BUJ, met Rupert.
Circa 1997 – Formed dum dum with Rupert Anderson and Steve Dixon. We were briefly called 'pop'. Club Montepulciano.
Circa 1998 - Silicone EP by dum dum. Met Lucy.
December 2000 - Moved to Koln.
January 2001 bought BH
August 2001 - Returned to Lewisham from Koln.
December 2002 - Boomerang by dum dum finished.
September 2003 – Started at Sturgis Associates.
Circa 2004 – Khali joined band, Rupert left, replaced by Joe.
January 2005 - I move back into WC. Lady Luck Club & Nino.
July 2005 - Met Vicky.
Circa 2005 - Formed Cake Boy with Ed Hoskin and Jennie Swain later renamed the Chandeliers. Ed and Jennie quickly left, I continued with Steve, then Milla and Joe.
Circa 2005 - Dirge (with Steve Dixon, Joe Hoover and Kahli Gaskin).
January 2006 - Album 1 by the Dirge finished. Did bass & backing vocals.
Joe suggested Milla could be a good bass player for the Chandeliers – she was!
February 2006 Left Sturgis Associates, started at ABA.
Performed at Standon Calling festival and Koko around this time.
November 2006 – Moved to Halesworth with Vicky. Started at Spparc.
December 2007 - Queen of Hearts by the Chandeliers finished.
2008 – Global financial crisis.
April 2009 – returned to ABA.
July 2009 – bought Herne Bay.
August 2010 left ABA for second time.
November 2010 – Started at CZWG.
Summer 2011 - Chandeliers finish Get Happy EP.
November 2011 - Married Vicky.
October 2012 - From The Swamp by the Chandeliers finished.
Summer 2013 - Gypsy festival.
December 2013 sold Herne Bay at huge loss.
June 2014 – Moved to Brighton. Johnny born.
August 2014 - Create Beauty EP by me and Joe Hoover.

September 2014 – Bought WS.
Oct 2014 - sold LG.
March 2016 - Tascam finished.
May 2016 - Iris born.
Summer 2016 – Brexit vote.
February 2017 Left CZWG and joined Yelo now living and working in Brighton.
2017 – Published 'Brexit - How the nobodies beat the SOMEBODIES' on i2i.
Feb 2019 - Left Yelo.
Jan 2020 - SJT.
February 2020 – C19 virus.
May 2021 – Kaylin born. Published 'BK&O'.
October 2022 – Started at Willow
2023 – Demiurge published political pamphlet (HTMTWMS).
2023 – Published 'the John Handley Songbook'.
January 2024 – John Handley died.
June 2024 – Published 'the Sebastian Handley Songbook'.
2024 – Published 'Rude Design' first edition.
October 2024 – Kasandra published TPOI.
January 31st 2025 – Moved to 2SR

Printed in Great Britain
by Amazon